The CREATURE
FROM THE SEVENTH GRADE

BOY OR BEAST

The CREA FROM THE BOY OR BEAST

VIKING

An Imprint of Penguin Group (USA) Inc.

TURE

SEVENTH GRADE

by **BOB BALABAN**

illustrated by **ANDY RASH**

VIKING
Published by the Penguin Group
Penguin Young Readers Group, 345 Hudson Street, New York, New York 10014, U.S.A.
Penguin Group (Canada), 90 Eglinton Avenue East, Suite 700, Toronto, Ontario, Canada M4P 2Y3
(a division of Pearson Penguin Canada Inc.)
Penguin Books Ltd, 80 Strand, London WC2R 0RL, England
Penguin Ireland, 25 St Stephen's Green, Dublin 2, Ireland (a division of Penguin Books Ltd)
Penguin Group (Australia), 250 Camberwell Road, Camberwell, Victoria 3124, Australia
(a division of Pearson Australia Group Pty Ltd)
Penguin Books India Pvt Ltd, 11 Community Centre, Panchsheel Park, New Delhi – 110 017, India
Penguin Group (NZ), 67 Apollo Drive, Rosedale, Auckland 0632, New Zealand
(a division of Pearson New Zealand Ltd.)
Penguin Books (South Africa) (Pty) Ltd, 24 Sturdee Avenue, Rosebank, Johannesburg 2196, South Africa

Penguin Books Ltd, Registered Offices: 80 Strand, London WC2R 0RL, England

First published in the United States of America by Viking, a division of Penguin Young Readers Group, 2012

10 9 8 7 6 5 4 3 2 1

Text copyright © Balaban & Grossman, Inc., 2012
Illustrations copyright © Andy Rash, 2012
All rights reserved

LIBRARY OF CONGRESS CATALOGING-IN-PUBLICATION DATA IS AVAILABLE
ISBN 978-0-670-01271-8

Printed in the USA   Set in Goudy Old Style   Book design and student planner doodles by Jim Hoover

To Mariah and Hazel,
my two favorite creatures

—B. B.

To Frank,
my favorite seventh grader

—A. R.

CONTENTS

The CREATURE
FROM THE SEVENTH GRADE

BOY OR BEAST

PROLOGUE

THIS IS A STORY about how something truly extraordinary can happen to the most ordinary of people (which I happen to be). Even if you lived in Decatur, Illinois (where I actually live), and were twelve years old (which I am), and the craziest thing you had ever done in your life was watch *Return of the Jedi* five times in one day (which I actually did when I was nine)—even then, something truly extraordinary could happen to you.

Everything I am about to tell you is true. It's not "loosely based on," or "suggested by," or anything even remotely like that. I would swear on the lives of my seven turtles, but you probably wouldn't believe me anyway. I am still having a hard time believing it myself, and it happened to me.

Let me put it to you this way: if you suddenly became invisible and could fly and were able to teleport yourself to a planet inhabited by talking cheese balls over twelve trillion light-years away in less time than it takes to wash your hands, it wouldn't even come close to what I am about to tell you.

Before we go any further, here are a few things you should know about me: I am a seventh-grade student at Stevenson Middle School, grades five through eight. I am not exactly the most popular kid in my grade. Translation: if you rated my popularity on a scale of one to ten with one being the lowest and ten being the highest, it would be zero. Does that bother me? What do *you* think.

My big brother, Dave, is a senior at Stevenson Upper School, grades nine through twelve. He is so popular it hurts. He is tall, gets invited to everything, and was recently voted Most Likely to Succeed in the annual yearbook poll.

Dave is Chief Justice of the Student Court. He has

three girlfriends. Plus he got early acceptance to his favorite college (Michigan State). And did I mention that he's really nice, isn't at all stuck-up, and is great at every sport known to man plus a few you have probably never even heard of like "Frisbee golf" and "water polo"?

Well, I'm only twelve, so I'm not all that interested in three girlfriends and early acceptance to college at this point. But other than that, do I wish I could be more like Dave? Let me put it to you this way: *duh*.

Craig Dieterly is my nemesis. His hobbies are burping, dropping water bombs, and making my life miserable. He is the president of the seventh grade (he ran on a platform of "Vote for Me or I'll Hurt You"). He's captain of everything. Football. Baseball. Soccer. The world. You name it. He is six feet three inches tall and weighs about thirty million pounds. If his brain were a state it would be Rhode Island.

Craig Dieterly has been picking on me since the day I entered Stevenson Lower School in prekindergarten. He used to terrorize me on the playground. Once he wouldn't let me get off the whirl-and-twirl and kept spinning me around until I threw up. Another time, in the sandbox, he stole my pail and shovel and refused to give them back until the head of the entire Stevenson Lower School, pre-kindergarten through grade four, threatened to call the police.

In homeroom our desks are in alphabetical order. My last name happens to start with a "D." It's Drink-water. Don't laugh. So every morning I have to sit next to this Craig Dieterly guy. We have a deal: I sharpen his pencils and do his math homework, and he doesn't steal my lunch money. Unless he feels like it. He refers to me as "Snow White's little-known eighth dwarf, 'Brainy,'" when he refers to me as anything.

In case you were wondering, my full name is Charles Elmer Drinkwater. (What were my parents thinking?) I hate my middle name so much even my best friends don't know what it is. **PLEASE DO NOT TELL ANYONE.** When I was eight I tried to have it legally removed from my birth certificate, but you're not allowed to alter official records until you're over eighteen. I checked. If Craig Dieterly ever finds out my middle name is Elmer, I will have to relocate to another solar system.

Did I mention that my voice hasn't even begun to change, so when I answer the phone people still say, "Can

I talk to your mother, little girl?" Embarrassing but true.

Oh, and I don't do sports. Call me crazy, but I try to avoid getting squished or maimed or humiliated whenever possible. Last year Principal Muchnick made a rule that all middle school boys had to join the middle-school football team. I told him it was my constitutional right to refuse to play a sport that could cause premature death.

Principal Muchnick doesn't like it when students disagree with him. He told me to quit bellyaching and join the team. He said it would make a man out of me. I told him I thought I was a little small to play football.

That is a gross understatement. There are beagles I know that weigh more than I did. In fourth grade I nearly blew away in a strong wind. Both feet were off the ground and I was halfway down the block by the time I managed to grab hold of a fire hydrant. Alice Pincus, the littlest girl in my class? Last year Norm Swerling dared her to pick me up and carry me to the end of the hallway outside of language lab. She didn't even break a sweat.

Needless to say, Principal Muchnick prevailed and I joined the team. My father had to order custom-made shoulder pads for me because they didn't come in my size.

In the first quarter of my first and last game I caught the ball by mistake and three defensive linebackers the size of refrigerators came running after me. I was so scared I fainted before they could tackle me, and Nurse Nancy had to give me smelling salts and carry me to her office to recover. Try living that one down.

Mom always said I should drink my milk, take my vitamins, and be patient. She promised me that I would eventually go through some kind of "magical transfor-

mation" and sprout like a weed and I wouldn't have to get my clothes in the little boys' department anymore. Guess what? Mom was right.

My story begins at three o'clock in the morning one cold and windy Monday in October. It is not for the faint of heart. Don't say I didn't warn you.

Notes:

Remember to give Craig Dieterly my lunch money if I want to live to see thirteen.

Grr! Yargh!

Pew! Pew.

Ask Mrs. Adams why she only gave me a 96% on my paper.

I can help, Amy

My hero!

Ask Amy Armstrong if she needs help with her math homework.

1

THE JOURNEY BEGINS

IT'S THE MIDDLE of the night. I awake screaming in a sweaty, heart-stopping panic, gasping for breath, legs tangled in the sheets. I've had this nightmare before. Seven times in the past seven days, but who's counting. Dave mumbles "shut up" from his bed on the other side of the room and goes back to sleep faster than you can say "little brothers are a serious pain in the butt."

The dream always begins the same way. First my face turns green. Then I get scales all over my body. Next my toes transform into hideous, long, webbed things that taper into razor-sharp toenails. By the time the gill slits begin to form at the base of my ever-lengthening neck, I scream and wake up. Just your plain old recurring "I'm turning into the Creature from the Black Lagoon" dream.

Creature happens to be my favorite monster movie. The scene where the creature skulks around in his lagoon and watches mild-mannered Dr. Reed's beautiful girlfriend, Kay Lawrence, swimming just above his head is a classic. I give it eleven goose bumps out of a possible ten on the fear-o-meter. It is an official "Monsterpiece" in my book.

My dad says that if you have a vivid imagination and you go around watching scary movies before you go to bed, you have to be prepared for a certain number of bloodcurdling nightmares. It comes with the territory.

But this isn't my imagination. I know it. Just as sure as I know that E equals mc^2. So I drag myself out of my nice warm bed, quietly tiptoe over to the bathroom, doing my best not to wake Dave again, and try to tell myself that the clammy sense of dread I'm experiencing is from staying up too late watching *Poltergeist* and *Rosemary's Baby*.

Still shaking, I peer into the mirror. The circles under my eyes are definitely darker. But then, if you woke up in the middle of the night for the last seven days in a row, the circles under your eyes would be pretty dark, too. And my skin *has* taken on an alarming greenish caste. After careful scrutiny, I chalk it up to the fluorescent bathroom lighting and shuffle back to bed.

I remind myself that it was just a dream. But try as I might, I am unable to shake the feeling that life as I know it is about to come to an end.

IT'S NOT THAT EASY BEING GREEN

MY SCIENCE TEACHER, Mr. Arkady, stands in front of first-period science class and slowly writes the word HERPETOLOGY in big script letters across the blackboard. He looks and sounds exactly like a vampire. If I didn't know for 100 percent certain that Bela Lugosi was dead (I saw his grave in a documentary on the SyFy channel once), I would swear he had returned as a Stevenson Middle School teacher and taken over Mr. Arkady's body.

I asked my mom to get me transferred out of his section when school started this year because I didn't want to have a vampire for a teacher, but she just said I'd have to deal with it. I'm glad she made me, because he turned out to be one of my favorite teachers. (But I still wouldn't want to run into him in a deserted alley on a dark and stormy night.)

"Who knows vut that vurd means? Hands, please," he says, gliding back to his desk, humming a haunting melody, and carrying an ancient leather-bound notebook in his long bony fingers. There is a rumor floating around that Mr. Arkady keeps a running total in there of all the people whose blood he has sucked and turned into vampires, along with their vital statistics—height, weight, hair color, and exact moment of death (or undeath).

In my opinion, Mr. Arkady is a really great teacher. He has a good sense of humor, he encourages us to think on our own, and he always has time to talk to us about our problems. The fact that small children run screaming at the sight of him is not his fault.

"Surely somebody knows the meaning of that vurd."

A sea of blank faces stares back at him.

I know exactly what herpetology means (it's sort of a hobby of mine, actually), but I am much too busy staring at my hand to raise it. It's all dry and cracked looking.

And it has the same dull greenish tinge that it had in my nightmare last night. Hmm.

Lucille Strang, one of my best friends, raises her hand. Lucille knows the answer to just about any question you could think of asking and isn't bothered one bit by the fact that the rest of the class thinks she's a know-it-all. Because basically she does know it all.

Lucille has an IQ of about forty million and a mouth so jam-packed with braces that it's virtually impossible for her to get through a metal detector without an intervention from the National Guard. At six feet one and a half inches, she is the tallest girl in the entire Stevenson School District, grades prekindergarten through twelve, and, as far as I can see, the tallest girl in all of Decatur, Illinois, population 76,122.

At Stevenson Middle School if you're a boy and you're really tall, you get three extra points on your popularity scorecard. If you're a girl it's at least ten points against you. If you're Lucille and your hobbies are experimenting with fruit flies, playing with your ferrets, and learning about the space-time continuum, take off another fifteen.

What's up with my feet? They're all puffy and

swollen. They crowd the sides of my size-three sneakers like they're trying to escape. This is not a good feeling.

"Students, please, vair did you hide your brains today?" Mr. Arkady says, drawing himself up to his fullest height and hunching his shoulders like he's adjusting his bat wings before swooping down on an unsuspecting victim. "Surely somevun besides Miss Strang knows vut a herpetologist is."

Sam Endervelt raises his hand. He's my other best friend. It's a small subset. He's kind of round and really, really pale. He sort of looks like Gomez from *The Addams Family* except he's too young to have a mustache. A lot of people are scared off by Sam's freaky, ultralong dyed purple hair. He's sort of pre-Goth. Like he's not all the way there yet, but he paints his fingernails black and wears a fake nose ring. He also sings soprano in the school chorus because even though he's six months older than I am his voice hasn't changed yet, either. He's harmless. I swear.

If I'm a geek, Sam's an off-the-charts supergeek. He says the number on his popularity scorecard is so low it's unlisted. Sam knows a lot about popularity scorecards. He should. He invented them. There's no actual card or anything. As Sam is quick to explain to anyone who will listen, it's a humorous way of demystifying popularity that makes it seem silly and unimportant. Guess what? It doesn't work. Uh-oh. My calves are starting to tingle. Like when you've been sitting in one position for too long and your legs are about to fall asleep. Only I haven't been sitting in one position for too long. Did I mention that my tongue is also up to something funny? It feels thick and lumpy and dry.

Sam pokes me in the back. "What's with your neck, pal?" he whispers. "It looks like it's got mold growing all over it."

"I have no idea," I whisper frantically.

"I guess that's what happens when you don't wash behind your ears." He chuckles. For a moment I wonder whether I'm getting some kind of weird cosmic payback for my inattention to personal hygiene. "You're starting to look like Jeff Goldblum in *The Fly*."

"If you ver a herpetologist . . ." Mr. Arkady continues as he scans the room for someone to call on. (He's actually 35 percent less likely to call on you if you raise your hand. I keep track of stuff like that.) "Vut ting vood you know a lot about . . . uh . . . Amy?"

Amy Armstrong, the most popular girl in Stevenson Middle School, grades five through eight, and possibly the universe, looks up distractedly. "Gee, I'm drawing a blank."

"Perhaps if you and Rachel Klempner paid as much attention to vut I am sayink as you do to the notes you are passing to each udder, maybe you vood know vut is goink on in this class."

Amy Armstrong gives Mr. Arkady a dirty look.

Rachel Klempner, on the other hand, smiles cheerfully, like Mr. Arkady has just paid her a great compliment. She pretends to like everybody to their faces, and then she goes around behind their backs and says terrible things about them. In fifth grade she started a rumor that Lucille and Sam and I had a contagious disease that caused us all to have really bad hair. No one would sit next to us for weeks.

Rachel has been going out with Larry Wykoff since last year. She wears this stupid ring he gave her to commemorate the day he first texted her. It looks like it came out of a Cracker Jack box, and it's made out of plastic. Once it got lost during gym period, and she almost had a nervous breakdown and had to be sent to Nurse Nancy's office.

Rachel and Amy are members of the One-Upsters, a seventh-grade clique dedicated to the proposition that all middle-school girls are definitely *not* created equal, and the ones with better clothes and even better hair really are . . . well . . . better.

One-Upsters can usually be found hanging with Banditoes, their male counterparts. Banditoes, like Craig Dieterly and Larry Wykoff, are great at sports, care deeply about their sneakers, and tend to have fewer pimples than everybody else. Banditoes and One-Upsters wouldn't be caught dead talking to Mainframe weirdoes. Namely Lucille, Sam, and me.

We Mainframes are happy to hang with anybody who is willing to hang with us. Nobody's exactly lining up. Well, actually, on the first day of school this year, Alice Pincus asked if she could be a Mainframe, and of course we said yes because (A) we think it's rude to reject people who want to join your clique. And (B) nobody ever wants to and it's pretty embarrassing having a clique with only three people in it. But after she hung with us for a few days, Alice Pincus ditched us and went on the waiting list to become a One-Upster.

"Take a vild guess, Miss Armstrong." Mr. Arkady

isn't about to give up. "Vut does a herpetologist do?"

What's up with my shoulders and my neck? It's like my insides are rearranging themselves. It doesn't exactly hurt. But I wouldn't recommend it, either. I ache everywhere. I am definitely coming down with something. If this continues I will have to go see Nurse Nancy for sure.

"I think I know!" Amy says excitedly, like for once in her life she might actually have the answer to a question besides "What time does the party start?"

"I believe a herbologist is someone who knows a lot about different kinds of cosmetics. And herbs." Amy smiles beguilingly at Mr. Arkady, then goes back to reading Rachel's note.

"It's *herp*etologist, Miss Armstrong." Mr. Arkady is clearly not beguiled in the least.

Suddenly I get such a severe cramp in my right arm that I start waving it around in the air.

"Mr. Drinkvater, vill you please put us out of our misery and tell us in vut field you vood be an expert if you ver a herpetologist?"

"I would know all about amphibians and reptiles, like snakes and turtles and lizards," I blurt out, lowering my right arm and massaging it with my left. I really do feel sore. I hope I'm not getting the flu. Halloween is Friday. It's my favorite holiday, and I don't want to miss it. Last year I went as Frankenstein. This year I'm either going as the Invisible Man or the Mummy.

"Derivation, if you please, Mr. Drinkvater," Mr. Arkady asks.

"The word 'herpetologist' comes from the Greek word 'herpeton,' which means things that crawl," I say as I hold the back of my hand to my forehead to see if I'm running a fever. I don't feel warm. I feel cold and clammy. "Like Herman, for example."

I glance over at Herman the iguana, who usually spends his time lazing in the corner of his cage under the relaxing glow of his basking lamp. He suddenly begins to pace around his little enclosure like a convicted felon trying to break out of the slammer.

Herman's looking over at me like he's just laid eyes on a long-lost friend. He makes happy little chirping sounds and jumps up and down trying to attract my attention. *Sit, Herman. Stay.*

"Good goink, Charlie," Mr. Arkady says, slinking back to the blackboard.

My legs feel like someone is rubbing them with sandpaper. I pull up my pants a couple of inches and check out my ankles, which are slowly but surely turning wrinkly and green right before my eyes.

"Speekink of things that crawl," Mr. Arkady says, smiling at the class and revealing his sharp, pointy incisors, "today you vill select a topic for your report on 'herpeton' from the followink . . ." As he speaks he writes on the blackboard:

FROGS, TOADS, NEWTS, SALAMANDERS,
TURTLES, LIZARDS, SNAKES, CROCODILES

"You vill present a detailed analysis of the animal of your choosink. Matink habits. Genealogy. Dietary needs. Funny facts. By the time I am through vit you, you vill be junior herpetologists yourselves. . . ."

Everything about me seems like it's getting just a little bit bigger. My pants are tighter. My shirt collar bites into my neck like a noose. I've heard of growth spurts, but this is ridiculous. It's like I'm in *The Incredible Shrinking Man*, except instead of getting smaller, I'm getting bigger. And greener. And scalier. It's only first period, and my popularity scorecard has already plunged a good ten points. I'll be into triple negative digits by lunchtime if this goes on much longer.

"Projects vill be due in vun month, and vill be graded on accuracy, depth, and originality," Mr. Arkady says. "Tink out of the box. Amaze me."

Herman is so excited he writhes ecstatically in his cage. He knocks over his water container and stands on top of it, struggling to climb over the side of the terrarium.

"What's with Herman?" Sam whispers.

"Yeah, it's like he's having some kind of an attack," Lucille adds.

"What did you have for breakfast, Charlie?" Sam asks. "Your breath smells like seaweed."

Lucille sniffs the back of my head. "Yeah, and your neck smells like dirty socks." She sniffs some more.

"Hey, that tickles," I say. "Cut it out."

Herman makes a sudden, high-pitched squealing noise, takes a running jump, and practically flies out of his cage in one long, graceful motion. He has sensed the presence of the other scaly critter in the room. And it's me. Herman comes bounding over two full rows of desks and leaps into my arms.

"Bad Herman," Mr. Arkady says sternly. "Back in your cage this minute."

Herman pays no attention. He nuzzles his face against my shoulder and makes soft cooing sounds as he licks my cheek.

"Looks like Drinkwater finally found someone to appreciate his inner beauty," Larry Wykoff says drily. When he isn't busy being Rachel Klempner's idiot love slave, Larry is humor editor for the school paper, *The Sentinel*. He plans to be a famous comedy writer when he grows up. He calls himself "Mr. Funny," and I hate to admit it, but he sort of is.

"Mr. Drinkvater, please return that igvana back to his cage immediately," Mr. Arkady orders. "Vee vill not tolerate playink vit animals durink class."

"Yes, sir," I reply. All eyes are on me as I stumble over my expanding feet and nearly drop Herman on his head when I return my scaly friend to his terrarium.

"You walk like you play football, Charlie Lancelot Drinkwater," Craig Dieterly says. He has been trying to guess my dreaded middle name ever since he figured out I hated it. This was in second grade, when we all had to sit in a circle and call out our middle names, and when it got to me I said I didn't have one.

"That's not it," I whisper back.

"How 'bout Melvin?"

"Uh-uh," I reply, and hit my knee on Mr. Arkady's desk. The shiny red apple that Rachel Klempner brought him this morning rolls off and hits the floor with a thud. I am so mortified I would dig a hole and crawl into it if I could. "I'm really sorry, sir," I say, sinking into my desk chair. "I'm just not myself today."

"What a relief." Craig Dieterly chuckles.

"That's not nice," Lucille whispers.

"Nice is for sissies," Amy replies, applying a fresh coating of lip gloss to her bright-red lips.

"Does it come naturally, or do you have to work hard to be such a total dweeb, Drinkwater?" Norm Swerling asks.

"Takes one to know one," I retaliate, and then instantly regret it. You can't win with these people. Don't even try.

"Look who's talking," Craig Dieterly pipes up. "It's Snow White's other little-known dwarf, 'Pathetic.'" He points at me and laughs.

Dirk and Dack Schlissel, Neanderthal-sized identical twins, and fellow Banditoes, laugh along with Craig Dieterly. The Schlissels have huge bodies and tiny heads. What they lack in intelligence they more than make up in brute strength. Sam and I can never decide if they each have their own separate brain (we don't think so) or whether they share a common one (much more likely).

"Quiet in the classroom!" Mr. Arkady barks. "Not funny, Mr. Dieterly."

Sam takes out a magnifying glass from his fanny pack and studies the back of my head intently. "If I didn't know better, Charlie," he says under his breath, "I'd say you were undergoing a series of dramatic molecular changes on the cellular level."

"Oh great," I murmur.

"I'm really worried about you," Lucille whispers. "You should see a specialist."

"In what?" I reply. "Herpetology?"

Suddenly I can feel my teeth getting longer and sharper. My neck grows longer, too. And skinnier. I stare, transfixed, at my fingers as each of my hands morphs into a claw with three sharp talons. My toenails burst through my sneakers. I cross my legs and try to hide my lower extremities under my desk. It's my nightmare come true: I, Charles Elmer Drinkwater, am turning into the Creature from the Black Lagoon.

3
ROCK AROUND THE CROC

RI-I-I-I-I-NG! That's the bell, and not a moment too soon. I grab my backpack and lurch out of the crowded room in a blind panic, leaving Sam and Lucille in my wake. I cover my face with my notebook and hurtle through the noisy hallway to the service stairs. I push open the metal door and begin the steep ascent to the roof. I have no idea what I'll do when I get there. I only know I can't let anybody see what is happening to me.

I hear Sam behind me, huffing and puffing, trying to catch up. Sam is built for sitting and eating. Not running. "Hey, wait for me!" he shouts.

"Me too!" Lucille cries. "Slow down!"

I wish I could. But the change is fully upon me now, and a desperate animal instinct to flee has taken over and propels me up the steps three at a time. With every passing second I feel my bones lengthening, my joints realigning, and scales multiplying to cover my expanding body. I am literally bursting out of my clothes. Pieces of my shirt hang in shreds around what used to be my waist.

By the time I reach the third floor my spindly neck has grown so long I have to stoop to keep my head from hitting the ceiling. Rows of spiky ridges erupt all over my scaly green body faster than I can count them. My formerly matchstick-thin legs are growing into massive coils of bone and sinew, like drumsticks on a steroidal chicken.

As I burst onto the roof, a long and powerful tail suddenly explodes from the base of my spine, causing me to lose my balance, nearly sending me tumbling back down all the way to the basement.

Sam arrives, gasping for breath. Lucille is close behind, panting and holding her side. They stare at me, too stunned to speak.

I look down. My tiny feet have blossomed into

webbed green flippers the size of platters. I reach up to what used to be my forehead and realize I no longer have a face. In its place a long bony ridge connects my enormous crocodile-like jaws to my sloping cranium.

Forget about being popular. At this point I would happily settle for human.

The sun breaks through the clouds, slashing a blinding white-hot ray across my enormous green body. My scales sparkle and glisten. My transformation is complete. The monster lives. I throw my long neck back, open my jaws to the sky, and cry, "I am the Creature from the Seventh Grade!"

Sam runs his pudgy fingers through his dark purple hair and shakes his head in disbelief. He rubs his eyes. "Charlie, is that really you?"

"Unfortunately, yes," I say in my easily recognizable, high, squeaky child's voice. I have the body of a ferocious monster but I still sound like a little girl.

"Wow!" Sam exclaims. "You look just like the Creature from the Black Lagoon, except bigger. If Wes Craven only knew. He could direct the sequel, and you could star in it, and you wouldn't even have to act! Think of all the money they'd save on makeup and prosthetics."

"Don't get too worked up about it, Sam," I reply. "I'm sure this whole transformation thing is only temporary."

"We're taking you to Nurse Nancy's office right now." Lucille heads for the door to the stairs. "Let's go."

"What's she going to do about it?" I ask. "School nurses aren't even allowed to give you *aspirin*. They can't do anything."

"He's right," Sam adds. "I got sent to Nurse Nancy's office with a splinter last week and she couldn't even touch it. All she could do was take my temperature and put cool compresses on my forehead."

"We have to do *something*," Lucille says. "We can't just stay up here on the roof all day twiddling our . . . um . . . claws."

"Maybe we slipped through a wrinkle in the space-time continuum," Sam says. "And we're all in some kind of alternate universe."

"OMG!" Lucille exclaims. "I've only been trying to find out if the space-time continuum exists as more than just a pure mathematical construct for my whole life! Can you imagine if we just stumbled into it during Arkady's class? Wouldn't that be thrilling?"

"Yeah, thrilling." I am not exactly convinced. "Why

don't you guys hide me in the utility closet next to Principal Muchnick's office and go figure out what's happening to me and make it un-happen?"

"Good thinking," Sam says. "We'll go search for 'spontaneous mutation in the adolescent Homo sapiens' on the Internet. We could try to decode your genome if we could find an electron microscope."

"I've always wanted to get my hands on one of those things," Lucille confesses.

"My uncle Leon knows someone who works at NASA," Sam says eagerly. "I bet we could borrow one of theirs."

"Are you serious? Call him right now." Lucille is practically jumping up and down. "This is so exciting I can't stand it."

"I don't want to be a buzz kill or anything," I say, "but do you think you guys could concentrate on getting me off the roof before somebody sees me, or would that be too much to ask?"

"Sorry, Charlie," Lucille replies. "I didn't mean to get carried away."

I point to a discarded packing blanket lying in the corner by the trash. "Why don't you wrap me up in that thing and lead me to the closet?" I ask.

"Consider it done!" Lucille says as she grabs the blanket and throws it over my head. "We'll get you back to your old sixty-eight-pound weakling self so fast your head will spin." My two friends lead me to the door to the back stairs.

"I can't wait," I say as I bang my head on the ceiling. "Ouch." I keep forgetting I am so tall. I tear a hole in my blanket with the tip of my pointy claw so I can see where I'm going, and we hurry down to the second-floor landing together.

Sam opens the door to the hallway. Lucille pokes her head out and looks around cautiously. "The coast is clear," she whispers. "Let's run for it!" My enormous flippers make a loud flapping sound as they smack against the linoleum.

"Keep it down under there, Charlie," Sam whispers. "Everybody'll hear you."

As if on cue, Alice Pincus comes scurrying around the corner, heading for the girls' room, and nearly bumps into the three of us. "What're you guys doing in the hallway?" she demands. "You're supposed to be in English. You missed attendance. Everybody's looking for you. Where's Charlie?"

"We can't tell you," Sam says. "It's a secret."

"What do you have under those blankets?" Alice continues. I hold very still.

"Guess," Lucille answers.

"I bet it has something to do with Halloween," Alice announces proudly.

"I bet you're right," Sam says.

"Is it scary?" Alice asks.

"Extremely," Lucille replies.

"Goody," Alice chirps. "I love being scared."

"Then you're in for a real treat," Lucille says.

"We have to go," Sam says. "We're late."

It is getting very warm under my blanket. Alice heads for the bathroom, and we continue down the hall to the utility closet. Sam opens the door and I quickly step inside, knocking over a pile of dictionaries with my tail. A box of old erasers falls on my head. Clouds of chalk dust billow in the air.

"Stay put," Sam orders. "And don't worry. You'll be you again. I promise."

"Are you sure?" I ask.

"Absolutely," Lucille replies confidently. "Someday we'll look back at today and have a big laugh about the whole thing."

"I hope so," I say. "Because I'm sure not laughing about it now."

"Shush," Sam orders me as he shuts the door. "Think positive thoughts."

I listen to the clatter of my friends' footsteps as they race down the corridor. I stand alone in the dark closet, trying to come up with a single positive thought. *I won't have to spend a lot of time shopping for a Halloween costume this year* is the only thing I can come up with. The dust from the chalk is making my eyes water and irritating my very large nasal passages. I try not to sneeze.

Suddenly the door to my hiding place flies open and Rachel Klempner is standing in front of me. I am so startled I scream and drop my packing blanket. Which makes Rachel Klempner scream. And then I scream again.

"What . . . who . . . how . . ." she stammers, shaking her head in disbelief.

While I try to think of something reassuring to say, the tickling in my nostrils becomes unbearable and I can control myself no longer.

Achoooooooooooooooooooooooooooo!!! The force of my sneeze blows Rachel Klempner backward across the hall. She nearly crashes into a wide-eyed Alice Pincus, who is returning from her trip to the bathroom.

"It's me. Charlie Drinkwater," I explain meekly. "I transformed."

"You are the scariest thing I ever saw in my whole life," Alice squeals. "I love it. I'm telling everybody." And then she races back to Mrs. Adams's English class.

Before I have a chance to catch my breath, a bunch of excited seventh-graders are texting and pointing their camera phones at me. "What's it like to have flippers?" Norm Swerling asks. Amy Armstrong wonders if it's okay to touch my tail. Rachel Klempner asks me if I bite. I am so mortified I shut my eyes and pretend that I'm invisible.

You know that dream where all of a sudden you're walking around school in your underwear and everybody in your entire grade is staring at you? Well, this is exactly like that dream, only about THREE HUNDRED AND FIFTY MILLION TIMES WORSE!!!!!!!!!!!!!!!!!! Plus it's really happening.

Sam and Lucille hear all the commotion and come racing back just in time to see Principal Muchnick emerge from his office, clapping his hands together loudly. He's dressed in his usual three-button suit. His oily black hair is slicked back neatly. His pine-scented aftershave enters the hallway before he does. He's fat enough to make a believable Santa Claus every year at the middle-school holiday assembly. But not a very jolly one. Everyone hurries back into the classroom when they see the principal. Except me.

"Come with me this instant, young . . . um . . . whatever you are," he says, and a minute later I'm standing in his office, trying to explain that the enormous webbed and scaly green creature with the long, floppy tail pacing nervously in front of his desk really is Charlie Drinkwater.

"It's me, Principal Muchnick," I plead. "My brother, Dave, got early acceptance to Michigan State. My parents' names are Fred and Doris. I'm a founding member of the local chapter of Junior Scientists of America. I was born on August sixteenth. I live at four forty-two Lonesome Lane. Look. It's all here in black and white," I say as I hand him my student ID.

"Ever hear of a little thing called identity theft?" Principal Muchnick says, eyeing me suspiciously. "How do I know you're not a dangerous monster pretending to be Charlie Drinkwater?"

"If I were a dangerous monster, wouldn't I be out

on a rampage, killing innocent people and knocking over buildings or something?" I protest.

"Maybe . . ." Principal Muchnick refolds his pocket handkerchief into a perfect triangle.

"If I were a dangerous monster, why would I be standing in front of your desk, carrying a book bag, holding a number-two pencil in my claw, and trying to convince you that I am an unpopular seventh-grader in Stevenson Middle School, grades five through eight?" I continue. "What would be the point of that?"

"Heaven help me, I believe you." Principal Muchnick sighs. He hands back my ID. "Leave it to you to pull a stunt like this." Principal Muchnick has had it in for me since the time I complained to him about being on the football team. To this day he thinks I fainted on purpose. Believe me, I didn't.

"Okay. So what do I do with you now, Charlie Drinkwater? School guidelines specifically forbid bringing animals onto school property without a properly executed pet authorization form. You don't happen to have one of those conveniently tucked away in that backpack of yours, do you?"

"No, sir," I reply. "I'm afraid I don't."

He pulls a large volume marked *Rules and Regulations* from his bookshelf and searches through its contents. He reads intently, shaking his head and *tsk*-ing under his breath. The furrows in his brow deepen.

"Is there a problem?" I ask.

"It seems there is some doubt as to whether a student needs an official pet authorization form if the pet in question also happens to be the student." Principal Muchnick sighs again, puts the book away, and picks up the telephone. "In situations such as these, there is only one thing to do."

"What is that, sir?" I ask nervously.

"Phone your parents and tell them to pick you up immediately." He begins to dial. "And then I will call an emergency session of the local school board to discuss your, shall we say, *precarious* situation." He drums his fingers absentmindedly on his desk and waits for someone to pick up.

"Why, hello there, Mrs. Drinkwater," he says at last. "This is Principal Muchnick. I have some rather unusual news for you. Are you sitting down?"

4
HOME SWEET HOME

IT'S THE MIDDLE of fourth period. Sam and Lucille get special permission to leave math class early so they can wait with me in front of school for my mom to come and pick me up. A couple of kids hang out windows and stare down at me, transfixed, until their teachers pull them back in again. An awkward silence hangs in the air. Sometimes it's hard to know just what to say when your best friend turns into a giant lizard.

"I almost forgot," Sam says. "Mr. Arkady told me

to give you this." He hands me a small envelope. I rip it open with the tip of my claw and read the neatly written note:

Dear Mr. Drinkwater,

    Please make an appointment to see me at your earliest convenience. I would like to discuss your upcoming report and share a few of my insights with you regarding amphibians, the class to which you apparently now belong.

It's much easier to understand what Mr. Arkady is saying when he writes stuff down.

"What's he want?" Lucille asks.

"He wants to talk lizard with me." I place the letter carefully into my backpack. "My mother is totally going to lose it when she sees this tail." I wave it around for emphasis.

"Probably." Lucille ducks and narrowly avoids getting hit in the face.

"Not to mention what she's going to do when she spots your claws and your flippers and your gill slits," Sam says, fiddling with his fake nose ring. Sometimes it slips off when he gets excited and you have to pretend not to notice while he reattaches it.

"We left no stone unturned," Lucille says. "We want you to know that."

"We looked all over, but we couldn't find a single thing about spontaneous mutation in the human adolescent," Sam says. "We were online during most of English class."

"I thought Mrs. Adams was going to send us to detention," Lucille adds. "And then Sam pretended he was going to the bathroom and went and called his uncle Leon."

"But he couldn't help us out because he lost his friend at NASA's phone number," Sam says.

"You did your best," I say. "What more could you do?"

"I figured maybe you walked into a cloud of radiation and insecticide by mistake," Sam says. "Like Scott Carey in *The Incredible Shrinking Man*."

"I thought of that, too," I reply. "Only I didn't. I would have remembered."

"Yeah. That's what Lucille said."

"We did an extensive search on SpaceWeather.com

for signs of recent meteor showers, extreme sunspot activity, or unusual lunar occurrences," Lucille says. "Renegade electromagnetic forces have been known to cause some pretty unusual effects on people. Look at the Wolfman."

"But we didn't even come up with even one measly little asteroid," Sam says.

"We checked out more than a dozen UFO Web sites," Lucille continues. "We thought maybe you had a Close Encounter of the Third Kind and got turned into an alien. We found some pretty credible recent sightings in Ohio. And a couple in Wisconsin," she says. "But not a single sign of recent extraterrestrial activity in all of central Illinois, I'm sorry to report."

"So what do you think happened to me?" I hear the *putt-putt* of my mom's old red pickup truck rounding the bend as it slowly approaches school. "Slowly" is its main speed. Its only other one is "even slower."

"We have absolutely no idea," Lucille admits. "But there's lots of places we haven't even heard from yet. We're still waiting for Ripley's Believe It or Not! to call us back, for example."

"We're not giving up," Sam adds.

"Of course we're not," I say. "We're Junior Scientists of America. We can figure out anything."

"Whatever happens, I have two words of advice for you, Charlie," Lucille says as my mom drives up. "Wear deodorant."

Mom's truck lurches to a halt in front of the building and backfires loudly. Several times. You wouldn't want to enter any races with our truck, but it's good for hauling around stuff and for quick trips to the grocery store. And picking up your son from school when he turns into the Creature from the Seventh Grade.

"Hey, Charlie!" my mom calls out cheerfully. "Hop in the back. You're waaay too big to ride up front with me."

"Your mom seems to be handling the situation awfully well," Sam whispers as I pull down the tailgate and haul my massive body onto the truck bed. My tail is so long that it hangs over the side, nearly touching the ground.

"I don't get it," Lucille says.

"She probably knows how to fix me," I say hopefully. "She's really good at repairing stuff."

"All aboard!" Mom shouts.

"Call you later," Lucille says as she slams shut the tailgate and hurries back to class.

"Ditto," Sam yells.

"Double ditto," I cry back.

"So long, kids," Mom hollers, and I hunker down as she tries to pull away.

"Tries" is the operative word here. The engine whines and strains. And then dies. She turns the key to start it again, and I can feel the gears grinding as she shifts into neutral and back into first. And we're still not budging. I am much too heavy for this old truck to handle. You can smell the oil burning in the carburetor. A thin trail of black smoke rises up from under the hood. I pray no one takes a picture of this and posts it on the Internet.

Just as I am about to give up hope of ever moving, the engine finally turns over, and the truck starts up. I look back at my school getting smaller and smaller as we chug down the road. I hold on to the sides of the truck with my claws to keep from falling out. It's really bumpy back here.

When we stop at the light on the corner of Fifth and Lonesome, passersby gawk at me. I greet them with a cheery wave of my tail and a friendly "It's me, Charlie, only big and green," hoping to avoid a panic in the streets. It's not working. Our neighbor Mrs. Pagliuso stares at me so hard that she walks right into a tree. A terrified babysitter pushing a buggy grabs the baby in her arms when she sees me and runs off in the opposite direction.

Before you can say, "My son looks like something that just escaped from Jurassic Park," we're in our drive-way, pulling up to the garage. Balthazar makes a mad dash out of his doggy door, barking an enthusiastic hello, before he takes one look at me, screeches to a halt, and heads for the nearest tree. In five seconds flat, my ninety-five pound Labradoodle is halfway to the top, clinging to a branch for dear life and howling like a wounded banshee.

My mom gets out, marches over, lowers the tailgate, and waits while I maneuver my enormous hulk of a body onto the lawn and head for the house. As I walk I leave giant webbed footprints in the grass.

"You run inside and scrub those claws and I'll go put on a big pot of hot cocoa," Mom says. "Your father will be home soon. We'd like to have a little chat with you, honey."

Mom holds the kitchen door open and motions for

me to come in. I am so tall I have to stoop over so the top of my head doesn't crash into the door frame. I am so wide I have to squeeze myself through the opening.

Just as I get inside, my dad's bright-yellow Toyota careens around the corner and races up the driveway. Dad jams on the brakes, jumps out of the car, and runs toward the house.

"I thought I'd never get here." He hugs Mom and hangs his hat on the doorknob.

"Look who's here, Fred," Mom says, pointing at me.

"Good to see you, son. You're looking very green." And with that my dad gives me a big smile and a pat on my big green slimy shoulders, like he's used to seeing giant green scaly creatures in the hallway on a regular basis. When he thinks I'm not looking, he wipes the creature goo from his hand onto his pants leg and we all head for the kitchen.

I accidentally whack my dad on the side of his head with the tip of my tail as I turn to wash my claws in the sink. He moans quietly and clutches his ear. "Sorry, Pop," I say, wiping my claws on one of mom's favorite dish towels and trying not to rip it to shreds. "I'm having a little trouble getting used to my tail."

"Who isn't?" my dad says jovially, as he drags out the sturdy wooden milk crate my mom uses to store her cookbooks, pulls it up to the kitchen table, and gestures for me to sit down.

Mom carries over mugs of steaming sugar-free cocoa with miniature nonfat marshmallows floating on top. "Careful, Charlie," she warns as she sets them on the table. "It's awfully hot."

I stick out the first few feet of my enormous tongue and carefully lap up a little of my favorite hot beverage. "Can I get you some cookies?" Mom asks.

"Yes, please." I try not to sound too eager, but I am ravenous.

When my mom comes over with a freshly baked batch of her famous low-calorie butterscotch melt-aways, I quickly spear the bite-sized treats with the tip of my pointy tongue and shovel them into my cavernous jaws.

Mom's a great cook. She runs a catering business for people on restricted diets called Slim Pickings. She works out of the house. That's how come she was home when Principal Muchnick called. Dad manages a sporting goods store downtown called Balls in Malls. He usually works late on Mondays. But apparently not this Monday.

"Manners, Charlie," Dad says under his breath as he sits down next to me and hands me his handkerchief. I take it in my claws and politely dab at the crumbs clinging to what passes for my mouth.

"I think it's time we had our little chat, sweetie," Mom says, smoothing the front of her dress and taking her seat at the table. She gives Dad a gentle poke in his side with her elbow. "Don't you think so, Fred?"

Good. This is the part where my parents explain what's happening and tell me everything's going to be all right.

Dad takes a big gulp of hot chocolate, sets his mug aside, and looks me squarely in the eye. "Charlie, your body is going through some pretty big changes," he begins.

"Yeah. I noticed," I say, holding up both my claws and waving my tail at him.

He continues, unfazed. "Changes that may have cause you to feel embarrassed, self-conscious, awkward, and out of control. Do you catch my drift, son?"

"I caught it."

"Your mother and I want to assure you that these changes are a perfectly normal part of growing up and becoming an adult," Dad says matter-of-factly.

"They are?" I ask, stunned.

"Absolutely, honey." My mom gently takes one of my claws in her hands, careful not to cut herself on its knifelike edges. "Welcome to adolescence, Charlie."

"*That's* what this is?"

"There comes a time in every young man's life when he undergoes . . . uh . . . a certain, shall we say, life-altering process," my dad explains. "Only in some cases, the process happens to be a little more . . . uh . . . life-altering than others. Like . . . um . . . yours, for example." My dad always gets nervous when he has to talk about personal stuff. He would much rather talk about baseball. Or the weather. Or anything.

"I would really like to know what's happening to me, Mom. I don't understand what Dad's trying to tell me."

"The facts of life," Charlie," Mom replies. "Plain and simple."

I thought I was already pretty well informed about this whole "facts of life" business. Boy, was I wrong. The "facts of life" are neither plain nor simple. At least not in the Drinkwater household.

5

THE BIRDS AND THE BEES AND THE MUTANT DINOSAURS

ACCORDING TO MY father, the Drinkwater "facts of life" began nearly sixty million years ago, when a cataclysmic meteor shower struck the earth with such force that it wiped out most of the dinosaurs on the planet. "But a few hardy specimens from a little town that just now happens to be called Decatur, Illinois, survived and underwent a dramatic mutation," Dad explains.

"Can you imagine, Charlie?" Mom says. "The only remaining dinosaurs in the whole world lived in our own backyard? Isn't that amazing?"

"I guess so," I reply weakly. I am getting more confused by the minute.

"Before they died, these brave creatures laid eggs containing genetically altered baby dinosaurs, son," Dad continues. "And when they hatched, the babies turned out to be amphibians."

"Do you know what an amphibian is, Charlie?" my mother asks.

"Of course I know, Mom," I say impatiently. "We're studying them in science class. They can live in water and on land. Salamanders are amphibians. What does any of this have to do with me?"

"I'm getting there," Dad says, "hold your horses. Those mutant dinosaur babies survived their hostile environment by heading straight for the bottom of the lake that had been formed when one particularly large meteor landed near their swamp. That's Crater Lake, Charlie."

"Crater Lake! Can you believe it, honey?" Mom exclaims. "We took you there to learn how to swim when you were just four. You loved that place."

For the record, I hated it there. Too many mosquitoes, the sand got stuck between my toes, and it smelled like rotting logs.

Mom continues. "And then sixty million years later, one adventurous young female mutant got tired of life underwater, swam to the surface of the lake, and climbed out onto the shore. She discovered she could breathe air as well as water, so she decided to stay."

"Quite a story, Charlie, don't you think?" my dad asks.

"Yeah. Very interesting. I only have one question. **WHY ARE YOU TELLING ME THIS??????**"

Mom says, "You see, that adventurous young female mutant creature grew up to become your grandmother, Nana Wallabird, may she rest in peace."

"What?" I gasp. "Nana was a *dinosaur*?" I am so stunned I nearly fall off my milk crate. "Why didn't anybody tell me?"

There is a long, awkward silence before my mom answers. "We thought it would upset you." She speaks so softly I can barely hear her.

"You thought it would upset me, so you didn't tell me my grandmother was a dinosaur!"

"A mutant dinosaur," Dad quickly adds. "There's a big difference."

"She wasn't as large as a regular dinosaur," Mom explains.

"Just how large was she?" I ask. Nana died when I was only two. I don't remember her very well.

"About your size, I'd say." Dad measures the air with his hand. "Seven or eight feet. I'm not really sure. Maybe . . . uh . . . nine."

"That's pretty large," I say.

"Yes, but she carried herself like she was smaller," Mom says. "She was terribly graceful."

"And very attractive," Dad remarks. "As mutant dinosaurs go."

"Can you tell me why Grampa Wallabird married a mutant dinosaur, or will that upset me too much?" I ask.

"Your grandfather had a heart as big as Texas," my dad explains. "And a nose to match."

"With feet the size of banjoes," my mom chimes in. "Not to mention the hump on his back. And that chronic skin condition."

"Are you trying to tell me that my grandfather was so funny looking only a mutant dinosaur was willing to marry him?"

"Basically," Dad admits.

My mind is racing as I try to process all this new information. "Okay," I say. "So I have a little dinosaur DNA in my genome. I guess that explains why I turned into one. But maybe it's just temporary. I could be the Creature from the Black Lagoon for Halloween and then change back into myself for Thanksgiving. I mean, stranger things could happen. They already did. Right, Mom?" I'm beginning to feel a little better.

"Don't get your hopes up, honey," Mom replies.

"Why not?" I ask.

"You won't be changing back," she says. "Trust me. I know."

"But how do you know, Mom?" I persist.

"Parents know these things," she says quietly.

"Take it from your mother, Charlie," Dad says. "She knows."

"You mean I'm going have to stay this way permanently? As in forever????????? With scales and a tail and gill slits . . . and . . . and . . . everything?" I wail.

"Yes," Mom says softly. "Now you're upset."

"Upset????????? Mom, they don't even have a word for what I am. All this time you knew I was going to turn into a mutant dinosaur and you never even mentioned it?????????"

"That's the thing, honey," Mom says, wringing her hands. "We didn't know for sure it was going to happen, so we decided to spare you the unnecessary anxiety. We told your brother that he had a recessive mutant dinosaur gene, and he was so traumatized he failed math and practically got himself kicked off the baseball team."

"And after all that, he never even grew flippers or a tail or anything," Dad explains. "So we kind of assumed . . ."

"We assumed your recessive mutant dinosaur gene would stay recessive like your brother's," Mom says. "Until we got that call from Principal Muchnick today." Mom turns away from me, her eyes well up, and she starts to cry.

"How am I going to face everybody? What am I going to tell them? 'Being the shortest boy in the entire middle school wasn't bad enough, so I had to turn into an overstuffed chameleon'?"

Mom dries her eyes, blows her nose, and tucks her hanky back into her pocket. "So you're a little different. Big deal. Different is good. Nana Wallabird was different. And she had a wonderful life."

"She married a guy who looked like the Hunchback of Notre Dame," I say. I poke around at the marshmallows floating in my cocoa with my tongue. "I wouldn't exactly call that wonderful."

"Yes, but Grampa Wallabird loved Nana very much,"

Dad reminds me. "They were happily married for nearly fifty years."

"And Nana thought Grampa was the handsomest guy in the world," Mom says, pouring more hot cocoa into my cup. "Be glad you're not like everybody else, Charlie. You're one of a kind."

"I sure am. Craig Dieterly always says that when they made me they didn't break the mold, they arrested the guy who made it. I don't even want to think about what he's gonna say about me now."

"He's just jealous of you, honey. There are a million Craig Dieterlys in this world," my mom says. "But there's only one Charles Elmer Drinkwater. And don't you ever forget it."

"Do you have to say my middle name, Mom?" I complain.

"You're special, honey," Mom says. "Get used to it!"

"I don't want to be special!" I protest. "I want to be like everybody else. Who wants stupid old flippers and a tail and gill slits? Why couldn't I at least be a mammal, Mom? Or even a reptile? It's not fair!" I stomp my flippers on the floor so hard the chandelier begins to shake.

"You should thank your lucky stars, son," Dad says.

"With diversity like this, you could get a full scholar-ship to any university in the country. Maybe even . . ." he pauses dramatically ". . . Harvard. Who knows?"

"I don't care!" I wail. And stomp even harder.

"Harvard, Fred? Can you imagine? Our little pea-nut?" She begins to cry all over again. "Our little boy is finally growing up. It's all happening so quickly."

"I want to be human!!!" I scream.

My dad puts his arm around her. "If it's any consola-tion, Doris, emotionally he's still just a child."

Suddenly Dave clomps into the house, cradling his arm. "I strained my left wrist," he announces as he barges into the kitchen. "Can you believe it? Coach Grubman sent me home in the middle of the practice game. I have to ice it every fifteen minutes and apply heat in between. The play-offs are Thursday. I don't know what I'll do if I'm not better by then." He grabs an ice pack from the freezer, wraps it around his wrist, then looks up and suddenly notices me. "Hey, look who in-herited the Drinkwater family curse. Tough luck, bro."

"Yeah," I reply. I'm still so upset I could weep. Only it's totally uncool to cry in front of your big brother. "I was sort of hoping it was temporary."

"It's not," Dave says, tightening the Velcro straps on the ice pack. "Curses rarely are."

"We don't call it a curse, Dave," Mom says, putting down her hot cocoa. "Let's not make value judgments, sweetie. Charlie is special. We must learn to celebrate our differences. Don't lick the floor, Charles, it isn't sanitary."

I immediately stop picking up crumbs and reel in my enormous tongue. "Sorry, Mom."

"We're all unique in one way or another," Mom continues. "Your father went bald when he was still a teenager."

"Doris, please . . ." My dad hates it when anybody mentions his lack of hair.

"Never be ashamed of being bald, Fred. I love that shiny head of yours. You know why? Because it gives you character and makes you strong. Poor Al Swanson has the hair of a Greek god, and what good did it ever do him? He still can't sell his way out of a paper bag."

Poor Al Swanson sells baseballs, mitts, and Ping-Pong paddles at Balls in Malls, the store my dad manages. My mother has been calling him "poor Al Swanson" for so long I used to think his first name was actually Poor.

Mom goes over to my dad, puts her arms around

him, and gives him a big kiss right on the top of his shiny bald head. "Your father was the youngest assistant manager in the history of the company. He made head of regional sales before his thirtieth birthday, and if he had all the hair in the world I couldn't love him any more." She kisses his head again.

"Thanks, Doris. You can stop kissing my head now." Dad pretends to be fed up. He loves my mom a lot. He just doesn't like saying it out loud.

"Now that we're all done celebrating our differences, isn't anybody going to ask me about how my practice game went today?" Dave asks.

"How did your practice game go today, honey?" Mom asks.

"It doesn't count if I have to ask you to ask," Dave answers.

"How'd you do, son?" Dad asks. "I'd really like to know."

"I scored four touchdowns before my injury."

"Not bad, Dave," Dad says proudly. "Not bad at all."

"Yeah. I would have broken an intramural record, Pop, except for . . ." He points to his wrist and the ice pack.

"You boys go upstairs and start your homework while your father and I make dinner," Mom orders.

"And don't forget to put some heat on that injury," Dad reminds Dave.

"I'm all over it," Dave replies.

"If I don't get accepted back into seventh grade, do I still have to finish my homework?" I ask, picking up my crate and taking it upstairs with me.

"You most certainly do," Mom says. "Now shoo! Both of you."

6
GUESS WHAT'S COMING TO DINNER

"**WHAT A BUMMER, DAVE.** You must really be upset about your wrist," I say as we go upstairs to our room.

"Yeah," Dave replies. "But not half as upset as you must be about turning into a mutant dinosaur."

"I was the littlest nerd in my class. Now I'm the biggest. When you think about it, things haven't really changed all that much. Except for my tail. And being green. And a few other things."

"Can you help me turn on the hot water, little bro?"

Dave asks, heading into the bathroom. "I can't really use my hand and I've got to get some heat on this injury."

"Sure," I say. I put down the drain stopper, turn on the water, and wait for the basin to fill. "I'm sure you'll be better by the big game. You have to be. What would the team do without you?"

"They'd be fine," Dave says, lowering his arm gingerly into the water.

"No, they wouldn't," I say. "And you know it."

"You're right," Dave says. "Ouch."

I shuffle back into my room and hand my turtles a claw-full of dried flies. They start licking me with their little tongues and trying to get me to pick them up. They coo at me affectionately when I go over to my desk to start working on my social studies paper. My legs are too big to fit underneath, so I sit sidesaddle on my crate.

The phone rings. I have trouble picking it up with my claws. When I finally do I nearly poke myself in the ear. "Hey, pal, what's up?" Sam asks.

"Plenty," I reply.

"If that's Janie Belzer, tell her I'm putting heat on my injury and I'll call right back," Dave hollers from the bathroom. Janie is one of Dave's three girlfriends.

He likes them all, but Janie is his favorite. She has curly brown hair and a big smile, and her hobby is painting portraits of dogs.

"It's for me," I holler back. "It's Sam."

"Really?" Dave yells back, surprised. When the phone rings it's generally for him.

"Really," I reply. Then I tell Sam all about Nana. And the family curse.

"Wow. That is so cool," Sam says. "I'm jealous."

"Don't be," I say. "It's not as exciting as it sounds." Sam wants to know if I'll be back in school tomorrow. "The school board still hasn't decided. If they don't let me back in it could be a real blemish on my record." Mom says colleges pay as much attention to your grades in stuff like "attitude" and "cooperation" as they do to your regular academics.

"If they don't let you back you could probably sue for discrimination against a minority. My aunt works at the American Civil Liberties Union." Sam's got relatives everywhere. "I bet we could get her to represent you."

While Sam explains the pros and cons of getting the ACLU involved in my case, I gaze absentmindedly at Dave's tropical fish, which are swimming in their large saltwater tank on the top of his desk. I wonder if Dave would mind if I ate just one? He might not even notice.

I wonder how it would taste with whipped cream on it. And a daikon radish with cilantro-flavored mayonnaise on the side. On a bed of udon noodles. I haven't eaten anything except cocoa and cookies since I became a creature. Hmm.

"Gotta go, Sam. Dinner's almost ready. Call you later." I hang up and casually amble over to get a better look at my appetizers. I am especially attracted to a family of five extremely rare blue-and-white-striped Egyptian mouth breeders swimming around a small plaster replica of Neptune's castle.

My dad says those fish look just like my uncle Marvin the mouth breather, my mom's sister Harriet's seventh or eighth husband. Only they live in Dave's fish tank on the side of his desk instead of in a split-level ranch house at 63 Maple Drive. And they don't have bad breath.

The phone rings again. I pick it up.

"Sam just called." It's Lucille. "I'm dying to hear all about your family curse."

"If that's Melanie, tell her I can't talk right now," Dave yells from the bathroom. "Tell her I'll call back."

Melanie Lindstrom is Dave's second-most favorite girlfriend. She is tall and has a long auburn ponytail, and her hobbies are rock climbing and collecting snow globes.

"It's for me," I reply. "It's Lucille."

Dave doesn't say anything. He shuts off the water and walks back into the room, looking annoyed.

"I have to lie down for a few minutes." Dave goes over to his bed. "Coach says I need rest. Think you could tear yourself away from that phone for a minute, sport?"

"Sure," I tell Dave. I ask Lucille to call back later, hang up, and find myself wandering to Dave's tropical fish again. "They're looking kind of hungry, Dave. I'd be happy to feed them for you while you rest."

"They're not hungry." Dave lies down. "I fed them this morning. Don't feed them, Charlie. The water gets cloudy if you give them too much."

"Oh yeah, I forgot," I lie calmly. "Why don't you take a nap and I'll wake you as soon as dinner's ready." Dave's fish beckon to me with their flashing tails and silvery fins.

Close your eyes, Dave. Go to sleep. You don't want to watch this. It's not going to be a pretty sight.

"How come you're staring at my fish?" Dave eyes me suspiciously. "Is something wrong?"

"I like to stare at fish," I reply. "It relaxes me." No, it doesn't. Staring at fish just makes me hungry. *I must not eat my brother's pets. I must stay far away from them.* But try as I might, I cannot seem to pry myself loose from that tank. I salivate at the thought of chomping down on those gleaming little beauties. The temptation is far too great. I can resist no longer. Somebody stop me. Noooooooooo . . . . !!!!!!!!!!!!!!!!!

Before I know what's happening, my head is underwater, and I'm snapping up angelfish and Bolivian rams in my powerful jaws like there's no tomorrow. The Egyptian mouth breeders cower behind their castle and manage to escape my mighty fangs.

"Back off!" Dave yells. He rushes over, grabs me by the haunches, and pulls me to the ground. He's really strong. Even with a strained wrist. He's not only the football team's star quarterback, he's also captain of the wrestling team. Now he gets me in a hammerlock, flips me over, and sits on top of my heaving chest. Boy, is he good.

"Spit 'em out, Charlie. RIGHT NOW!" Dave yells.

When I hesitate, he grabs my jaws in his hands and slowly manages to pry them open. He's struggling so hard the veins in his forehead are popping out. "Now, Charlie! Now! I'm not kidding." Dave is really brave. I wouldn't put my hands anywhere near my fangs if I were him. "Oww!" Dave screams. "My wrist!"

My parents hear the commotion and come running into the room to see what's wrong.

While Dave holds my jaws open, five of the cutest little fish you've ever seen come hopping out and onto the rug like they've just returned from an exciting vacation at SeaWorld. "They're still alive," Dave says. He breathes a sigh of relief, gets up, and flips the fish right back into their tank. They swim around happily, like they didn't just come within a whisker of total annihilation.

"You are going to have to learn to control those impulses, young man," my mom says sternly.

"I know, Mom." I hang my head. "I don't know what came over me."

"Apologize to your brother, son," Dad orders.

"I'm so sorry, Dave. This will never happen again. I promise. Are you all right?"

"What's happening to you, Charlie? Who is this big green scaly creature with the tongue that doesn't stop, and what the heck did he do with my little brother? The Charlie who I used to know is kind and gentle." Dave turns around and starts adjusting the pH balance in the tank like he can't bear looking at me another minute.

I'm not really sure who or what Charlie is now,

either. All I know is I'm starting to feel like one of those awkward, out-of-control adolescents who my parents and teachers keep talking about. If this is what being a teenager is like, I'm not so sure I want to be one.

Mom stands there and shakes her head. "Why don't you come downstairs and help your father and me with dinner, Charlie? Your brother needs some alone time."

Mom, Dad, and I go downstairs, while Dave stares silently at his fish tank, cradling his sore wrist.

7

I'M BAAAAAAAAAACK!

I BEHAVE MYSELF at the dinner table. I keep my tail from knocking into anything. I don't overeat. And I refrain from drooling on the tablecloth.

"Who wants an extra baked apple?" Mom asks. She has just finished serving baked caramel apples in a flaky pastry crust. Another one of her specialties. "I have one left."

"I do." I raise my right claw. "Unless you want it, Dave."

My brother just gets up from the table and brings

his plate over to the sink to scrape and rinse. He's been ignoring me since dinner started.

"You didn't touch your food, Dave," Mom says. "Didn't you like it?"

"I wasn't very hungry, Mom. Don't take it personally."

"Where are you going, Dave?" Dad asks.

"To put some heat on my wrist. And then to Lainie's house. I'm helping her with her advanced trig homework." Lainie Mingenbach is Dave's third-most favorite girlfriend. Lainie is captain of the cheerleading squad. She is very peppy. She has been studying jazz, tap, and flamenco since she learned how to crawl. "I'll be home by ten." And with that he is out of the dining room and down the hall before I have a chance to say good-bye. The front door slams loudly.

"I feel terrible, Dad. I didn't attack Dave's tropical fish on purpose," I blurt. "My animal instinct got the best of me. It won't happen again, I promise."

"I know that, son. And so does Dave. He just needs a little time to get used to you, Charlie," my father says. "That's all."

"He'll come around," Mom adds. "You wait and

see. He's going through some pretty big changes himself. Next year he'll be leaving home. And going to college. And living all by himself in a strange new city. Change is hard for everybody, Charlie. Big brothers included."

"If Dave thinks going to college is hard, he should try learning how to use a tail sometime." I flick the baked apple into my mouth with my tongue and swallow it whole.

The phone rings, and my father picks it up. "It's Principal Muchnick . . . shhh . . ." he whispers to me and my mother. "Uh-huh," Dad says into the phone. "Yes. I see. I understand. You are? Really? That's terrific. Mrs. Drinkwater will so pleased. Thank you for calling, Principal Muchnick."

"Good news!" Dad says as he hangs up the phone. "The board just voted five to four to let Charlie back into school. After 'careful consideration and reviewing all the facts' you are on 'provisional reentry,' son. Congratulations! Principal Muchnick says they're even having a special assembly in the morning to welcome you back and make sure your reintegration into the student body goes 'smoothly and without incident.' Isn't that thoughtful?"

"What does 'provisional reentry' mean, Dad?" I ask.

"It means that as long as you don't 'create a disturbance, interfere with the flow of normal school activities, break a school rule, or injure, maim, disfigure, or frighten anybody to death' for the next four days, you'll be allowed back in school permanently by the end of the week. You're really going to have to toe the line, son, because Principal Muchnick says if you don't you'll be suspended indefinitely."

"Isn't that wonderful, Charlie?" Mom exclaims.

"I don't like that 'provisional' part, Mom. I don't want everyone to go around judging me all week like I'm some kind of criminal. I'm self-conscious enough as it is. All I did was try to eat a couple of tropical fish. I don't see why everybody has to make such a big deal out of everything. Craig Dieterly is always creating disturbances and I don't see him getting put on provisional reentry. Why don't you just homeschool me and we'll e-mail in my assignments?"

"You're going back to school and that's that," Mom says firmly. "You're just going to have to get used to living in the spotlight, Charlie. You're one of a kind. You might as well learn to enjoy it."

The phone rings again. Mom picks it up. "Uh-huh. Uh-huh. I see," she says. She covers the mouthpiece with the palm of her hand and whispers to me and Dad, "It's Sally Pincus, Alice's mom. I never liked that woman."

Mom listens some more before she answers. "My son did not bite Mrs. Adams's ear off, Sally Pincus, and you know it. Honestly, must you believe everything you hear?"

Great, now everyone thinks I bite people. Take off another fifteen points from my popularity chart for violent behavior. Could it get any worse?

"Really? Well, I don't happen to care what Rachel Klempner's mother says." By now Mom is practically shouting into the phone. "Any parent who encourages their seventh-grade daughter to wear makeup and date boys is not someone I would consider a reliable source of information in the first place. Yes, well, you can sign petitions until you're blue in the face. It still doesn't make my son a menace to society. Because he isn't. Because I just know, that's how come," my mom says vehemently. "Charlie Drinkwater is the best-behaved young man in that whole school and I refuse to listen to another word of this nonsense." Mom slams down the phone.

Now they're signing petitions about me. I can't go back there. "Homeschool me, Mom," I plead. "I'm begging you."

Mom puts her hands over her ears and hums. "I can't hear you, Charlie, did you say something?"

Balthazar starts whining at the back door. It's time for his dinner. I go to the drawer in the kitchen table and take out one of his favorite liver snaps. I go to the back door, lean down, and hold it out in my claw. Balthazar will do just about anything for a delicious treat. Except, as it turns out, take it from me.

Dad goes over to let him in, but Balthazar refuses to enter the house until I hide around the corner where he can't see me, and Mom drags out an old stew bone, puts it into his bowl, and sets the bowl just inside the door. As soon as he finishes eating Balthazar sniffs the air and looks around suspiciously. I come out and wag my tail at him. I hold out my liver snap again. His tail stays tucked way down between his legs. He won't even look me in the eye.

He walks over and cautiously sniffs me with his big black nose.

"That's Charlie, Balthazar," my mom says. "You like

Charlie. Remember?" He looks back at her with a worried expression on his face as if to say, "Are you sure?"

"Charlie's your friend," Mom tells Balthazar. But he isn't buying it. He growls unhappily.

I hold out the treat again. He won't even sniff it. "Don't worry, Balthazar," I say. "You'll get used to me. Eventually. I hope."

Balthazar whines mournfully and slinks away.

"'Night, guys," I say.

My mom comes over and points to her cheek like she always does when she wants me to give her a kiss. "I'm waiting."

"Are you sure, Mom?" I ask.

"You're still my son, aren't you?" she replies. I lean my long scrawny neck way down and gently brush her cheek with the front of my jaws, being extremely careful not to snag her with my razor-sharp fangs.

"Where's mine?" my dad asks, and points to his cheek. "Don't I get one?" I lean over and carefully brush his cheek, too. And then I put the liver snap away and trudge upstairs to work on my social studies essay. My parents go into the kitchen to do the dishes. Dad stacks. Mom washes. He dries. They both hum.

Together they're like a well-oiled four-handed cleaning machine.

The first thing I notice when I enter my room is the big sign Dave has taped to his fish tank that says, DO NOT EVEN THINK ABOUT TOUCHING MY FISH. THIS MEANS YOU! in big red letters. I don't go anywhere near the tank. I head straight for my desk, pull up my milk crate, sit down, and go back to taking notes for my "José de San Martín and the Liberation of Argentina" essay that is due on Wednesday.

The phone rings. It's Lucille.

"Is Sam kidding, or was your grandmother really a dinosaur?" she asks breathlessly.

"He's not kidding."

"Wow!" she exclaims. "Are you okay? That is so intense."

"Define okay."

"Is the school board letting you back in school?"

"Yeah. As long as I don't scare anybody to death. I'm on provisional reentry."

"That's great," Lucille says.

"I guess so. Alice Pincus's mom is telling people I bit Mrs. Adams's ear off," I say. "Rachel Klempner's mom is sending around a petition to have me banned from school. Everybody hates me. I'm not so sure I want to go back."

"You can't go around worrying about what everybody thinks about you, Charlie, or you'll drive yourself crazy. Oops. Gotta go. My ferrets are squeaking. It's feeding time."

She hangs up and I try to calm down long enough to organize an outline for my essay. I am concentrating on José de San Martín's dangerous and challenging march across the Andes to liberate Peru. My premise is that San Martín was a heroic figure who succeeded despite great odds. The body of my essay will provide as many examples as I can find to support that premise. I will write the actual essay tomorrow night. Once you have a well-organized, comprehensive outline of your paper under your belt, the writing itself is a breeze.

When I'm done, I gather all my notes, along with my three-ring binder, my textbooks, my pencil case, an eraser, and some paper clips, and I arrange everything neatly in the backpack my parents gave me for my birthday last summer. It has special compartments for just about anything you can think of. It's very cool.

Then I browse the Internet for a while, looking for

fun and unusual local and national news items I call "factoids." I copy these items onto note cards I keep inside my pockets. I take them out and read them during those awkward silences that occasionally arise in certain social situations. Like when you come back to your school after you turn into a creature and everyone thinks you are a homicidal maniac. I call them my "social security blankets." I don't actually have any pockets to put my cards into at the moment. BECAUSE NONE OF MY CLOTHES FIT MUTANT DINOSAURS!

I hear a gentle tapping at my door.

"Honey, are you decent?" Mom asks.

"As decent as I'll ever be," I reply.

She opens the door and pokes her head into my room. Balthazar stands at her side, watching me. "I need to take a few measurements," she says as she walks in and takes out her tape measure, a pad, and a pencil. Balthazar won't set foot in my room. "Stand up and hold still, sweetie."

"What for?" I ask.

"I'm going to make you some school clothes, silly," Mom answers, as she begins to measure me. My chest is five feet around, my waist a whopping six. My tail is almost eight feet long. My mom's measuring tape isn't big enough to measure how tall I am. "Hmm." Mom sighs. "I hope I'll have enough material. Lean over, Charlie, I need to measure your head."

"Not a hat, Mom. Please," I beg as I bend my neck way down. "I look terrible in hats."

"Nonsense. You'll look adorable. Besides, I don't want you catching cold." She measures my head, earflaps included. "Okay. That's it." Mom gathers up her supplies. "See you in the morning, Charlie. Sweet dreams." She blows a kiss in my direction, then leaves my room and shuts the door behind her. I hear the clickety-clack of Balthazar's toenails in the hallway as he runs to catch up with her.

I get ready to go to sleep quicker than you can say "giant creatures don't have to lay out their clothes for school in the morning because they don't have any." I barely fit into my bed. I have to get up and push Dave's old camp trunk over, get my upper half under the covers, and rest my legs, flippers, and the last four feet of my tail on the trunk. It's not very comfortable, but what else can I do? I lie on my side (if you have a tail, it's the only way to go) and wonder if I'll ever get used to myself. I toss and I turn, but I can't seem to fall asleep.

Later, I hear Dave's footsteps on the stairs. He's back from Lainie Mingenbach's. He opens the door to our room slowly, tiptoes in, and goes to the tank to check on his fish. He breathes a sigh of relief when he finds them alive and well. Then he washes up, puts on his pj's, and gets into bed. Within minutes he is making Zs like a buzz saw in a tree farm.

Dave's snoring can be annoying sometimes, but tonight I find it reassuring. It's familiar. Unlike everything else in my new life. Dave breathes out. He breathes in. He snores. Out. In. Snore. Before I know it I am matching Dave, breath for breath. Slowly. Evenly. Out. In. Snore. In. Out. Snore.

The next thing I know, it's morning and my alarm clock is going off. I rub the sleep from my eyes and look around the room. Dave isn't in his bed. He must be downstairs having breakfast already. I'm starving. I stumble over to the bathroom to wash up.

Whoa. I almost trip over Dave's football. He promised Mom he wouldn't leave his stuff on the floor. I'll have to remind him. I look down at my feet. . . .

Wait a minute. Feet? I have feet? Yes, I do. Two of

them. Will you look at that! They're very small. And very white. Welcome back, toes! It's great to see you again. I look down at my claws, only they're back to being hands. Hooraaaaaaaaay!!!!!!!!! I race into the bathroom. I have to stand on my tiptoes to get a good look at myself in the mirror above the sink. Good-bye, fangs. Hello, teeth! Whoa. I have turned back into plain old, regular, ordinary . . .

Me.

I never thought I'd ever be so happy to see my funny little face again.

Boy, am I short. And skinny. My ears are even bigger than I remembered. Not for nothing did Uncle Marvin call me Dumbo until my mom threatened to stop inviting him for Thanksgiving unless he quit. For a second I actually miss being the biggest kid in my school and possibly the world. Which is when my alarm rings again.

Only this time it is my real alarm clock. Not the alarm clock in my dream. And this time I really do wake up. And this time when I run to the bathroom to get a good look at myself, I hit my head on the door frame because I am taller than Bigfoot. And this time when I look into the mirror, I have to duck way down to see my enormous, green, scaly head and almond-shaped, heavily hooded eyes staring back and me.

I am still the exact same creature I was last night. Only a little more rested. And a whole lot hungrier.

Notes: _____

The Schlissel twins
tied a tin can
to my tail—
subtract six
points from my
popularity card.

I'm a Freak!

delicious

Yum

sphere!

Do **Not**
eat Dave's
tropical fish
under **ANY**

circumstances!!

mmm

Don't forget
to give Craig
Dieterly my
allowance.

Ugh.

8
OH, BROTHER!

"DO YOU WANT bacon or sausage with those eggs, Charlie?" my mom asks, as she races around the kitchen making breakfast.

"Can I have both?" I ask.

"Why not?" she answers. "I must say, honey, your new outfit fits you to a tee."

"It's great. Thanks, Mom. I don't know how you did it." I'm wearing the clothes my mom made for me last night out of the fabric she was saving for new living room drapes. If you tried to design one outfit to make sure your son would be the laughingstock of his entire school, this would be it.

I'm wearing shiny green satin pants, a matching green satin cap, a green satin polo shirt (there's even a little green satin alligator sewn onto the pocket. I'm not kidding), giant green satin slippers, and a matching bright-green satin cape. It was supposed to be an overcoat, but Mom didn't have enough time to sew in the arms and put on the buttons.

I look like a cross between an Irish matador, the Jolly Green Giant, and the Incredible Hulk. But I know how hard my mom worked on my outfit. And I don't want to seem ungrateful. So I keep it to myself.

"How about you, Dave?" Mom asks.

"Bacon, please, and can I have some more milk, Mom?" Dave asks. "Coach Grubman says to eat lots of protein. The big play-off is only two days away."

"Coming right up." My mom wipes her hands on her apron.

Dave is still wearing his ice pack. He hasn't mentioned his strained wrist since he got up. I hope he's feeling better, but I'm not bringing it up if he doesn't. I don't feel like getting snapped at this morning. I'm already nervous enough as it is about "provisional reentry" and my welcome-back assembly.

"Anybody see my keys?" my dad asks as he hurries into the kitchen. "I know they're around here somewhere." It wouldn't be breakfast if my father didn't lose his keys.

"Your eggs are almost done, Fred," Mom says, heading for the stove.

"No time, Doris. I've got to catch the eight fifteen express to Champaign/Urbana. Big meeting with the head of national sales at ten. Can't be late. Now, if you were keys where would you be?"

"I would be sitting on the counter where you always put me." Mom sighs. "Not even a cup of coffee, Fred?"

Dad just points to his watch, grabs his keys, puts them in his pocket, and studies his reflection in the glass doors of the kitchen cabinets.

"How are you feeling this morning, Charlie?" Dad straightens his tie and adjusts his collar.

"Big," I say. "Really, really big."

"That's nice," he says. When my dad's in rush mode, you could tell him there was a purple aardvark sitting on top of his head and he wouldn't bat an eyelash.

"Bye, everybody." He gives Mom a peck on the cheek, flies out the door, and comes flying back instantly. "Oops. Forgot my briefcase." Mom just picks it up off the floor where he always leaves it and hands it to him silently, and off he goes again.

"You got a little bacon grease on your new shirt, Charlie," Mom says. "Hold still." She licks her napkin and starts dabbing away at the spot. "Did you get enough sleep last night?"

"Not really. Maybe I should stay home today. I'm not feeling very well."

"Really?" She puts the back of her hand on my sloping upper cranial ridge to see if I have a fever. "You do look a little green around the gills to me."

"He *is* green around the gills, Mom," Dave says. "Get used to it." He throws down his napkin and storms over to the refrigerator.

"Someone got up on the wrong side of the bed today." Mom goes over to Dave. "What's the matter, honey?"

Dave pours himself more milk and gulps it down before he speaks. "Dad didn't even ask me how my wrist was doing before he left."

"He meant to," Mom says, putting her arm around Dave's shoulder. "Your father has a lot on his mind, sweetheart."

"Well, so do I," Dave says, pulling away. "You can't believe the pressure I'm under. And nobody's asking me if *I* had a good night's sleep last night. Or sewing *me* special new green clothes, or telling me how great I look in them. Everything is 'Charlie this' and 'Charlie that.' 'How did Charlie sleep?' 'Does Charlie have a fever?' I don't know how much more of this I can take." He slams his empty glass down onto the counter. I have never seen my brother this upset.

"Honey, we're all under a lot of stress," Mom says. "I have to cater a luncheon for fifty crabby diabetics tomorrow, and Friday morning I'm doing breakfast for Mrs. Pagliuso's cousin's club and every last one of them inherited a gluten allergy. No French toast . . . no pancakes . . . don't even think about Belgian waffles. It's a nightmare."

"I'm really sorry, Mom. But what am I going to do if my wrist doesn't heal in time for the big game? We play the Barrington Bears on Thursday. I've been looking forward to being in the play-offs all year. It's just not fair."

"Honey, sometimes life gives us lemons," my mom

says, putting her arm around Dave's shoulder again. "And you know what? You've just got to get out your best pitcher and start makin' that lemonade."

Dave doesn't say anything. He just stands there looking lonely. And sad. And, although I never thought I'd be saying this, very little.

"Here, take my cape, Dave," I say. "Go ahead. It doesn't look that good on me, anyway. No offense, Mom." I lean over and place it on his big, broad shoulders, which are nowhere near as big and broad as mine. Mom gives me a grateful smile. I'm worried about Dave. I wonder how he feels about being shorter than his little brother.

"I know you want to make everything all right, Charlie," Dave says quietly. "But you can't. Thought you might want to know I injured my wrist again last night prying your jaws open." He hands the cape back to me. It's the first thing he's said to me all morning.

WAITER, THERE'S A DINOSAUR IN MY SOUP...

I AM FIVE minutes late for school. It wasn't my fault. My mother insisted on taking my temperature before she would let me out of the house, and when she discovered it was hovering at 73 degrees (well below the normal human average of 98.6), she panicked. It took several visits to YourPet.com and a personal phone call to our family veterinarian, Dr. Herbert Melville, before she could be convinced that I'm ectothermic (as are all fish, amphibians, and reptiles). So if the temperature in my house was 73 degrees, then mine should be, too.

I reach into my backpack to make sure I haven't forgotten my social security blanket cards, remind myself to look as harmless as possible, and walk up the stairs to Stevenson Middle School. I carry my milk crate in my claws, since none of the chairs at school could possibly fit me anymore.

I push open the front door with my powerful tail. Mr. Arkady floats smoothly across the deserted lobby. He waves his bony hand at me. "How about seventh period, sir?" I ask.

"I look forvard to seeink you then, Mr. Drinkvater!" He disappears into the assembly. There isn't a student in sight. I guess everybody's already in their seats.

Well, nearly everybody. Sam and Lucille come racing around the corner. "Everybody's terrified of you!" Lucille exclaims when she sees me. "Rachel Klempner told the entire class you bit Alice Pincus yesterday and then went on a rampage after Mrs. Adams told you no eating people on school property."

"Really?" I ask.

"Why else do you think they had to call a special assembly?" Sam replies. "You're the biggest thing to happen to Stevenson Middle School in years." Sam is so excited he tugs at his nose ring and it falls to the floor. Lucille and I pretend we don't notice him picking it up, like we always do when he drops it.

"What's that thing on your head, Charlie?" Lucille asks.

"It's a cap," I reply. "My mom made it for me last night. What do you think?"

"I think you should take it off," Sam tells me. He hides his nose with his left hand and clips the ring back into place with his right. "Fast."

"That bad, huh?" I ask.

"Worse," Lucille replies.

I remove my cap and put it in my backpack just as Principal Muchnick hurries down the center hall stairs looking unhappy. He has two main expressions: "stern" and "sterner." Right now he's way past "sterner" and approaching "if looks could kill."

"You're five and a half minutes late, Drinkwater," he says, looking at his watch. "I've been looking all over for you. This is not a very promising way to begin 'provisional reentry.'" I bet he just can't wait for me to goof up so he can send me home again. "Lucille and Sam: go right inside and find a seat. The place is packed to the gills. No offense, Drinkwater."

"No offense taken, sir."

"Come with me," Principal Muchnick orders. "Assembly is about to begin. You will be asked to say a few words. Keep your remarks succinct and to the point."

What remarks? Why didn't anybody tell me I would be called upon to speak? I would have prepared a few pertinent remarks. It's not bad enough I have to go stand in front of a crowd of people who hate my guts, now I have to say something to them?

"Move it, buster." Principal Muchnick leads me through the hallway that takes us to the auditorium's backstage entrance. We walk up a small flight of stairs, step onto the side of the stage, and pause behind the big red curtains. I can hear a low rumble of eager voices from the audience. The assembly is about to begin.

Speaking extemporaneously in front of large groups of people is not high on my list of favorite things to do. *Don't panic, Charlie. You'll be all right.* I take deep breaths and remind myself that we touched on public speaking briefly in Mrs. Adams's English class last fall. Mrs. Adams always told us to keep our speeches "informative, entertaining, and brief." I begin to sweat profusely.

I notice Dr. Craverly, the school psychologist, standing in the middle of the stage, anxiously tapping the mic with his finger. "Testing, one two three. Testing, one two three." The audience gets very quiet. "Before we start, I'd just like to say a heartfelt thank-you to . . ." Dr. Craverly stares at some notes he holds in his trembling hand. "To . . . to . . . to . . . I'm afraid I've lost my place." He tugs at his mustache with his free hand and begins again. "I'd just like to say a heartfelt thank-you to everyone who donated so generously to last week's winter coat drive."

Dr. Craverly hates speaking in public even more than I do. When he addresses large groups of people he gets so nervous he loses his place and starts pulling out his mustache hairs one at a time. He uses tweezers when it gets really bad. He puts the little hairs in a matchbox that he keeps in his desk drawer along with his car keys and a small bottle of something called Xanax, which Lucille says is for "anxiety disorder." Guess what? It's not working.

Lucille and I discovered his "hair in a box" collection last week in his office when we were rummaging around in his desk drawer for rubber bands for our perpetual motion machine. We almost barfed when we opened it.

What's he planning to do with all that mustache hair, anyway? Make it into facial wigs for people who don't have enough time to grow their own mustaches? My father says that having Dr. Craverly be the school psychologist is like letting the inmates run the asylum.

"A number of you kids have expressed your apprehensions about Charlie Drinkwater to me," he says, peering down at his notes. "I applaud your candor. I'd be lying if I told you I didn't share some of those very same concerns with you myself. Believe me, standing on a stage next to a mutant dinosaur is not my idea of a day at the beach." Dr. Craverly glances over at me. I wave my tail at him. He loses his place again. "But . . . but . . . but . . ."

At last he finds it. "But I can assure you the probability of Charlie Drinkwater going berserk and knocking us unconscious with one blow of his mighty tail and dragging us off to his lair in his powerful talons is slight. Although not entirely out of the question." He mops his glistening forehead with the handkerchief he keeps in his coat pocket. He looks at me again. If you listen closely you can hear his knees knocking together.

He continues reading. "As our thirty-second president, Franklin Delano Roosevelt, said so beautifully over seventy years ago, 'we have nothing to fear but . . .'" Dr. Craverly turns his notes upside down. He squints. He rubs his forehead. "I can't seem to read my handwriting . . . 'We have nothing to fear but . . . but . . . but . . .'"

As I listen to Dr. Craverly speak, here's what I think: *I couldn't do any worse than he's doing.* And I feel strangely reassured.

Just as Dr. Craverly reaches into his pocket for his tweezers and starts to pluck out his few remaining mustache hairs, Principal Muchnick strides over to center stage, pushes him to one side, and takes the microphone into his own hands.

"'We have nothing to fear but fear itself,'" Principal Muchnick says. "My sentiments precisely, Dr. Craverly. Now listen up, everybody. There have been a lot of rumors and innuendo flying around this place in the last twenty-four hours. Don't believe everything you hear. He may be big and green and scary looking, but Charlie Drinkwater is not dangerous. You can take it from me. He wouldn't hurt a fly."

A buzz of excited whispering runs through the crowd like an electric current. Principal Muchnick waits for the noise to die down. "He didn't try to bite Alice Pincus yesterday morning in the hallway during second-period English, either. And any stories you may have heard about his vicious attack on Mrs. Adams are just that. Stories." More whispering.

I am so happy to hear Principal Muchnick tell everyone the truth about me that I would be smiling a great big smile if I had lips.

"I'll tell you what, kids. Charlie's going to come out right now and tell us how he's doing in his own words." Principal Muchnick motions to me in the wings. "And you all can see for yourselves just what kind of a terrific kid he really is . . . I mean 'creature' . . . I mean . . . you know what I mean."

I feel strangely calm. And uncharacteristically confident. After all, how much can you expect from a mutant dinosaur, anyway? If I don't roar and eat a couple of people, I'm already ahead of the game. I leave the security of my red velvet curtains and walk slowly onto the stage.

There is a huge collective gasp the second everyone sees me. And then a hush falls over the room. Six hundred and forty-two pairs of eyes stare at me in rapt attention. It's so quiet you could hear a pin drop. And then Craig Dieterly's voice breaks the silence. "Quick. Somebody tell that kid it isn't Halloween yet."

"Quiet," Principal Muchnick commands in a steely voice. Craig Dieterly shuts up immediately. A few Banditoes snicker nervously.

The spotlight from the balcony suddenly hits me squarely in the eyes, practically blinding me. I shield my eyes with my claws. Mom warned me I was going to have to get used to being the center of attention.

Principal Muchnick motions for me to come to the center of the stage. *Don't be nervous, Charlie, you can do it. Relax your shoulders. Drop the tail tension. Remember to breathe.*

"Let's go, Drinkwater," Mr. Muchnick says firmly. "Now. We don't have all day."

I approach the microphone and carefully grasp it with my claws, raising it higher by several feet. Still, it barely comes up to whatever passes for my chin. *Remember, Charlie: Informative. Entertaining. Brief.* Here goes:

"First I want to thank Principal Muchnick and the whole school board for allowing me back on 'provisional reentry.' I promise I will do my best to live up to the confidence you have all shown in me." There is a smattering of polite applause. I informed. Now I will attempt to entertain.

"Thanks. I'm really happy to be here today. And a little . . . uh . . . surprised. Considering the pet show isn't for another three weeks." A few kids in the second row chuckle. It's not exactly a standing ovation. But it's encouraging. I continue.

"You know what? I am definitely going to enter that show. And if I don't win for biggest tail, I'm going to demand a recount." I wave my tail around to drive my point home. A few of the littler kids start to cry and have to be taken out of the room by their teachers. Although the rest of the audience does seem to be enjoying itself.

"Yesterday morning . . . boy, talk about your worst days ever. Somewhere between first-period science and second-period English, I turned into the enormous green scaly creature you see standing before you, complete with flippers, claws, a tail, five-inch gill slits in my neck, behavior problems, and an out-of-control appetite. Just think of me as your typical teenager. Only instead of acne, I get inflamed scales." I have to wait a full five seconds for the laughter to stop. This is fun.

"And when *I* get uncontrollable urges, I don't stay out past my curfew and party hard. *I* stay in my room and try to eat my brother's tropical fish. Ever feel like

you're having a bad hair day? Try having a bad *tail* day. Sometimes I can't get that sucker to do a thing I tell it to. I turn left. It turns right.

"On my way to school today, I had to yell at it. My own tail. I said, 'Tail, you're not the boss of me!' I grabbed it in my claws and forcibly restrained it and I still couldn't get it to listen to me. I tried to sit down when I got here today, and my tail stood up. Boy, was that embarrassing."

I'm getting used to the glare of the spotlight in my eyes. I can make out Sam and Lucille in the back row, smiling and giving me thumbs-ups. And what do you know—Amy Armstrong has actually stopped doing her nails for once in her life and is paying attention to me. And giggling. There's Larry Wykoff grinning as he scribbles notes on his pad. Rachel Klempner looks at him enjoying my speech and decides it's okay to enjoy it, too. A bunch of Banditoes gathered in the third row laugh and poke each other in the ribs. Even the Schlissel twins seem to be having a good time. Craig Dieterly isn't laughing. He looks extremely unhappy. This is really going well.

"Before I turned into a creature it's not like my face was so great or anything," I continue. "But at least I had one. Now all I've got is these two bulging eyes and jaws like a crocodile. With fangs like these, who needs teeth? My mother picked up one of my flippers this morning and tried to play tennis with it. I said, 'Mom, you're pulling my leg.' She said, 'Not hard enough!'"

Will you think less of me if I tell you I had them rolling in the aisles? Well, I did.

"So in conclusion, I would just like to say, the next time you see a big scaly green lizard creeping across your front lawn . . . say hello. It could be me. Thanks, everybody. You've been great!" I wave to the crowd, bow, and head for the wings.

Larry Wykoff puts down his pad and pen and applauds. A bunch of eighth-graders join in, whistling and stomping enthusiastically. A number of One-Upsters yell, "More, more!" Even Dr. Craverly stops pulling at his mustache hairs and joins in. Pretty much everyone except Craig Dieterly is clapping. He just stands by himself in the back and stares at all the people enjoying me and looks like he's about to throw up.

"Remember you're still 'provisional,' Drinkwater. I'll be watching you like a hawk. Step out of line and you'll be out on your tail so fast you won't know what hit you. I'm having Dr. Craverly draw up a special psychological evaluation of your recent behavior. We are keeping you on a very tight leash." Principal Muchnick leads me off the stage and back the way we came. "Don't let all that applause go to your head, Drinkwater. You were funny. But you weren't that funny."

I don't care what Principal Muchnick says. I rocked in there. Lucille is right. It's not what others think, it's what you think about yourself that's important. And I think I brought down the house.

As we exit through the stage door, Principal Muchnick scowls at me one last time and then hurries off to look for somebody to put in detention. Mr. Arkady glides over to me, smiling. "You are a good comedian, Mr. Drinkvater, I laughed like crazy. Beink a lizard brinks out your funny side. Don't forget to come and see me in my office today. I have sometink to say to you." He raises his bushy eyebrows and slinks gracefully away.

A couple of eager fifth-graders rush up to me. One of them gets up the courage to hand me a piece of paper and a pen. "Autograph please, sir?" he asks nervously.

"Don't worry, I won't hurt you," I say. "I just look dangerous." I sign my autograph with my right claw while trying not to rip the piece of paper with my left.

"I'd like to ask you a question," the boy asks. "If you

don't mind, sir." He speaks so quietly I can barely hear him. His friends draw closer, anxious to hear what I have to say.

"Fire away," I reply.

"My friends and I would like to know if you enjoy being a creature," he asks.

I have to stop and think for a moment. On the one hand I like the attention. And being taller than everybody else is cool. And it really seems to upset Craig Dieterly, which is pretty awesome.

On the other hand for the rest of my life I will be the only one of my kind walking the planet. A mutant dinosaur could get lonely.

"I wouldn't say I enjoy it, exactly," I slowly reply. "But I wouldn't say it's the worst thing that ever happened to me, either." I hand the boy back my autograph, careful not to scratch him with my claw.

The boy looks down reverently at the little piece of paper. He utters a barely audible "Thank you, sir." The bell rings and he and his companions race up the stairs, to share the exciting news of their Close Encounter of the Amphibious Kind.

Sam and Lucille come running over to me. "You

were great, Charlie," Lucille says. "We're really proud of
you."

"Yeah," Sam adds. "You killed."

"I did?" I say, worried.

"In a funny way," Sam explains. "Not in a Tyranno-
saurus rex kind of way."

Sam, Lucille, and I hurry up the stairs toward
English class. A bunch of middle-schoolers follow
close behind, whispering excitedly and pointing at me.
Alice Pincus pushes her way through the crowd to let
me know she thinks my tail is "way cool." "Great,"
I reply. "Be sure to tell your mom." Go figure. Rachel
Klempner practically steps on Alice Pincus to get closer
to me, says I'm a "gifted public speaker," and asks if I
have ever thought about having my own talk show. "It
was an honor and a privilege to be in the same room with
you, Charlie Drinkwater." When Rachel Klempner gives
you a compliment it's like getting licked by a cat. At first
it feels good, and then you can't wait for it to be over.

"C'mon, Charlie," Lucille says, nudging me. "Let's
go. We're late."

One of the Schlissel twins (they're not wearing their
baseball caps today so it's impossible to tell which one

is which) stops me to ask if I'd like to go toss a football around with him sometime. This is not exactly my idea of a great time. But when Dirk or Dack Schlissel asks you to do something, you don't say no. "Yeah, sure. Why not?" I reply. Evidently being a big hit at your own assembly can do wonders for your popularity scorecard.

Everyone wants to talk to me. And tells me how great I am. And asks me to hang out with them. A creature could get used to this kind of attention.

"Move your tail, Charlie," Sam says.

"It must be a terrible strain on you, Charlie," Lucille says. "All those adoring fans clamoring for your attention."

"Yeah," Sam agrees. "Better watch out or you'll get a swelled head, pal."

"You really think it could get any bigger?" Lucille jokes.

"Very funny, guys," I say. "Nothing's happening to the size of this head. These flippers are staying firmly planted on the ground."

"Good," Sam says. A smile flashes over his face and then disappears when Larry Wykoff approaches and asks if I'd be willing to do an interview with him this afternoon after sixth period for the front page of tomorrow's edition of *The Sentinel.* "Maybe," I say casually. "I'll have to check my schedule and get back to you after lunch." Translation:

"ARE YOU KIDDING!?!?!?!?"

10
FOOD FOR THOUGHT

THE LUNCH BELL is going to ring any minute. But I get a "special permission slip" to leave math class early so I can make it through the lunch line without creating a disturbance. Principal Muchnick says I'd better do everything I can to avoid any more "incidents."

Two Banditoes have already received demerits for spying on me during class and trying to take my picture through a crack in the door with their cell phones. In between third and fourth period, several eager sixth-graders approached me and offered to give me their lunch if I promised to sit next to them in the cafeteria. (I was so hungry I was tempted. You'll be proud of me, though. I didn't give in.) One of my fifth-grade fans tells me that he just sold my autograph to an upper-schooler for a dollar.

Even Norm Swerling asks if I want to go to the movies with him Saturday night. He never asked me to do anything before except help him clean all the blackboards once when he got punished for playing with his Game Boy during math. Norm Swerling wouldn't agree to be a Mainframe if his life depended on it. He is on the waiting list to be a Bandito. You have to be at least five feet four inches tall to be considered. If he grows another two inches he's a shoo-in.

I politely decline. Sam and I always go to Lucille's house on Saturday night and help her with her fruit fly experiments. It's really fun. Plus it's a tradition. Just like how every Wednesday night Lucille and I go to Sam's house for an early dinner. Sam's mom makes a wicked tuna noodle casserole and chocolate sundaes with rainbow sprinkles while we watch one of our favorite scary movies. And then we do our homework together. I wouldn't miss it for anything.

I know that I'm getting all this attention just because

I am the new mutant dinosaur on the block, but after a lifetime of being invisible, it feels good to be fussed over.

I hurry down the empty stairs to the lunchroom.

The cafeteria is nearly deserted. Mr. Arkady waves at me from the teacher's table on the side. "Seventh period, Mr. Drinkvater. Don't forget."

"I won't, sir," I reply. He sure seems anxious to talk to me. I wonder if he has some insight into my condition that I don't. He knows a lot about reptiles and amphibians.

A few lunchroom ladies stand proudly behind a row of delicious-smelling steam tables. I grab a tray and make my way over to the food line, where the aroma of freshly roasting wild Norwegian salmon hits me in the face like a brick wall. My pupils dilate. My jaws begin to quiver in anticipation. I haven't had a thing to eat since breakfast. I am *starving*.

Amy Armstrong runs in, grabs a tray, and lines up behind me.

"So like how strange was Dr. Craverly in that assembly today?" she asks. "Do you think he's losing it or what?"

This may not seem like a big deal to you, but it is the

first and only direct question Amy Armstrong has ever asked me since pre-K when she asked if I would move my tricycle because it was getting in her way. I am so astonished I nearly fall off my flippers.

It's one thing when a lowly fifth-grader asks for your autograph. But when the most popular girl in middle school and possibly the universe suddenly decides you are worth talking to, it is a **VERY BIG DEAL!!!!!** You have advanced at least five notches up the popularity scorecard.

The lunchroom lady asks me if I want the wild Norwegian salmon, the soup and sandwich, the chicken salad special, or the vegetarian entrée. "Um . . . I'll have the . . . um . . ." I am so flustered from Amy Armstrong talking to me I can't think straight.

"I don't have all day, kid," she reminds me, pushing her white paper lunchroom lady hat back on her forehead. The bell for lunch period rings. I hear the sound of thundering feet on the stairs. "What'll you have, honey?" the lunchroom lady asks Amy Armstrong. "Your finny friend over here can't seem to make up his mind."

"I'd like the chicken salad special," she says briskly. "Two scoops. No soup. Hold the roll, extra crackers on the side. Oh, and I don't do celery, so remove every single trace of it from my plate. I can't deal with stringy vegetables."

The lunchroom lady gives her a look and then very slowly starts picking bits of celery from the chicken salad with a tiny fork. I am getting hungrier by the second.

"I believe Dr. Craverly suffers from an obsessive-compulsive disorder, which is pretty strange, in my opinion," I say, wiping drool from my jaws with the green satin handkerchief my mother has thoughtfully placed in my pocket. "Because how can you be a school psychologist when you can't even cure yourself?"

"You're so right, Charlie Drinkwater. I never really thought about it that way before." And then Amy Armstrong suddenly looks right into my eyes like she is seeing me for the very first time. "You have an awfully interesting way of looking at things, did you know that?" Before I have a chance to respond she turns back to the lunchroom lady. "Do you think you could you pick faster, miss?" she asks. "I don't have all day."

The lunchroom lady rolls her eyes and picks even slower. If I don't get something to eat pretty soon I will keel over.

Lucille and Sam get into line behind us. "Hey there, Charlie," Sam says.

"Hey, guys," I reply faintly. On the one hand I am happy to see my friends. On the other hand I wish they would leave me alone so I could have a chance to talk to Amy Armstrong some more.

"I changed my mind," Amy Armstrong says. "I'll have the vegetarian entrée and a cup of soup." The lunchroom lady looks at her like she is about to dump the chicken salad over her head. "And could you hurry it up?" Amy Armstrong barks. "I have a special permission slip to eat early. I'm late for an extremely important appointment."

"What a coincidence," Lucille says sweetly. "Charlie and Sam and I have special permission slips to eat early because we're late for an extremely important appointment, too."

"I find that hard to believe," Amy Armstrong says coolly.

"And I find you rude, obnoxious, and arrogant," Lucille replies, equally coolly. Lucille has never liked Amy Armstrong, but she seems especially annoyed at her today. It occurs to me that my sudden rise in

popularity may be making Lucille a little uneasy.

"Ex*cuse* me?" Amy Armstrong snorts.

"Oh, ma'am?" Lucille says to the lunchroom lady. "This girl's extremely important appointment just got canceled. The big scaly green guy goes first. He'll have a double portion of the wild Norwegian salmon, please." By now the lunch crowd is beginning to pour into the room.

Amy Armstrong fumes while the lunchroom lady prepares me a heaping plate of salmon. "That's okay, ma'am," I tell her. "I can wait. I really don't mind. I'm not that hungry."

"Well, *we* sure are," Sam says, pushing ahead of Amy Armstrong. "C'mon, Lucille."

"What's the matter, Tubby?" Amy Armstrong says. "Afraid there won't be enough food left over for you and your creepy girlfriend?"

"You take that back or else," Lucille snaps.

"No way." Amy Armstrong grabs her tray and hurries off to join Rachel Klempner at her usual table in the back.

"Or else what?" Craig Dieterly has evidently overheard the tail end of our conversation. He storms over to our little group, puffs out his chest, and gets all red in the face. "You and Geico here don't scare me one bit, in case you didn't already know. Or else what, Metal Mouth?"

I would get right in Craig Dieterly's face and give him a piece of my mind if the very sound of his voice didn't make me want to run and hide. I can still hear him calling me "fraidy cat, fraidy cat" when he buried me up to my neck in sand and I started screaming on our excursion to Crater Lake in fourth grade. He threatened to leave me there overnight unless I promised to give him the Mexican jumping beans my uncle Marvin brought me back from Acapulco.

"Aren't you going to say something to him, Charlie?" Lucille asks.

"I sure am," I say nervously. "I say we all calm down, and go get something to eat."

Craig Dieterly looks at me like I am crazy. "And I say you'd better stick to your own kind or you won't know what hit you, Flipper, and I'm not kidding."

"What did I do?" I ask.

"Listen up, Newt Nose, and listen well," Craig Dieterly snarls. "You think you're such a big deal now that you have gill slits and a tail, but you're just a big green nothing. And if I ever catch you sucking up to, or talking with, or even looking at a One-Upster or a Bandito again, I will bring you a world of hurt. Don't think you can hide from me. I'll going to be all over you like white on rice." He lowers his voice. "Is your middle name Humperdink?" he asks.

"It's not," I reply. Craig Dieterly storms past me and knocks my tray of salmon onto the floor. "Oops. Clumsy me."

"You did that on purpose, Dieterly." I wipe salmon stains off my new green satin outfit.

"I sure did," he replies. "Want to do something about it?" Just then Principal Muchnick pokes his head into the cafeteria and stares at me with his beady little black eyes. "You try anything funny with me and I'll tell Principal Muchnick you hit me with your tail. You're on provisional reentry, Lobster Boy, and don't you forget it."

"C'mon, guys," Lucille says. "Let's go grab sandwiches from the vending machine and try to forget about these hopeless cretins."

Sam, Lucille, and I head over to the vending machine area and buy sandwiches, pretzels, Devil Dogs, and three big glasses of lemonade. Principal Muchnick stands in the front of the cafeteria tapping his foot and staring at me like I did something wrong.

We sit at our usual table in the back and talk about how unnecessary the Craig Dieterlys of the world are. And how unfair Principal Muchnick can be. And how much we admire José de San Martín.

"He was an officer in the infantry and fought against the Moors when he was only thirteen," Lucille says. "He must have been really brave."

"Yeah," I reply. "I bet *he* wouldn't have been afraid to stand up to Craig Dieterly."

"And you shouldn't be, either, pal," Sam says. "You're a mutant dinosaur. You're three times bigger than he is. You could rip him to shreds and eat him for breakfast if you wanted to."

"Fear isn't logical, Sam," Lucille explains. "My dog Fluffy weighs six pounds and fits into my mom's purse. And Balthazar is terrified of her."

"Yeah, but Balthazar is terrified of everybody," I remind her.

"I hate to say it, Charlie," Sam says, gulping down his third Devil Dog, "but so are you."

"True. And I'm not ashamed to admit it," I quickly

reply. "Because fear is sometimes a sign of superior intelligence."

"And sometimes it's just a sign that you're a coward," Sam says, burping loudly. "Excuse me."

"You're not excused," Lucille says. "That was gross. You just wolfed down your lunch faster than a mutant dinosaur."

"Well, excuse *me*," I say, picking up my empty lemonade glass and getting up. "I'm going for a refill."

As I walk over to the vending machine area, Amy Armstrong strolls by in the other direction. "Psst," she goes, and motions for me to lower my head. I look around for Craig to make sure he doesn't catch me breaking his stupid rules. Amy whispers into my ear, "You're way too interesting to spend your life hanging out with your Mainframe loser friends all the time. They're dragging you down with them into a bottomless pit of dorkitude and you know it, Charlie. Wake up and smell the coffee." She smiles mysteriously at me for a moment and then vanishes into the crowd.

My head feels lighter. My heart beats faster. I can hardly catch my breath. I guess that's what happens when the Amy Armstrongs of the world aim their smiles at you. It's like a secret weapon designed to make you forget how badly they have always treated you and your friends.

I refill my glass, go back to my table, and try not to think about Amy Armstrong as Lucille attempts to explain the space-time continuum to me and Sam for the ten millionth time.

"You guys . . ." This is what she always calls us when she is frustrated. "You guys, it's really simple: just think of time and space like they're all mixed up together in this one ten-layer coconut cake and you can't separate them. Okay?"

I don't understand what Lucille is saying but I'm getting extremely hungry for coconut cake. "So now imagine your knife represents time, and you slice a perpendicular cross section through the cake faster than the speed of light. The resulting coordinates formed where the knife meets the cake provide a continuous sampling of everything that is going on in the universe at any one exact moment. Are you following me so far?"

Nope. I'm thinking about Amy Armstrong. I wonder why I never noticed the dimple on her cheek before? I wonder whether she'll ever speak to me again. I wonder if there is a coordinate that represents lunch period and the precise moment in time Amy Armstrong smiled at me. I start to doodle on my paper napkin. I draw a graph. The horizontal lines represent the minutes in fourth period. The vertical lines represent Amy Armstrong. The intersecting coordinates represent . . .

"You're not even listening to me, are you, Charlie?" Lucille watches me coloring in my graph. "You're a million miles away."

I certainly am. I am on a planet in a distant galaxy where the most popular girl in the middle school and possibly the universe has just smiled at me. I like this planet.

11
NEWS AND CLUES

"TELL ME MORE," Larry Wykoff says, his pencil poised over his notepad. He adjusts the small portable microphone so it's closer to my jaws. "Tell me about the little boy inside the creature. How he feels. What he thinks about. His hopes. His fears. His dreams. I want to know everything."

Sixth period has just ended, and for the last several minutes I have been sitting on my crate doing my interview with Larry Wykoff for the school paper. Larry Wykoff is a Bandito. I don't want Craig Dieterly to catch me talking to him, so I asked to do my interview in the one place Craig Dieterly never ever goes: the school library. I don't think he even knows where it is.

Rachel "I'm pretending I like you but don't believe it for a second" Klempner sits across from me, next to Larry "I know more about humor than you ever will" Wykoff, and she hangs on my every word like she's actually interested in what I have to say.

"Awkward," I reply to Larry. "I feel really awkward. I'm always banging my head. And knocking stuff over with my tail. And tripping over my big, stupid flippers. Nothing fits me anymore. My bed. My desk. My clothes. The chair. You name it."

"I know the feeling," Larry says. "Believe me."

"You do?" It's hard for me to believe the popular "Mr. Funny" has ever had an awkward moment for one single nanosecond of his charmed existence.

"Sure. Who doesn't? Only the rest of us just *feel* like we're carrying around a big green scaly tail behind us. And you actually have one. That's some outfit, by the way."

"Yeah. My mother made it from this fabric she had left over from when she reupholstered all the furniture in the living room. It was supposed to be matching drapes.

When I sit on the couch you can barely see me."

"You have excellent comic timing," Larry Wykoff says, chuckling. "I never noticed it before. You remind me of Steve Martin in some of his early appearances on *Saturday Night Live*. Did anybody ever tell you that?"

All of a sudden Craig Dieterly's face appears in the doorway to the library. I never thought he'd find me in here. I get that sick feeling in the pit of my stomach I always get when the mummy burns his tana leaves in *Revenge of the Mummy* right before he stalks his victims. I stand up and start backing away from Larry Wykoff.

"Not in those exact words," I say quietly.

"Well, you do." He gets up and walks over to me, holding out his microphone. "Who or what would you say have had the biggest influence on your performing style?"

"My brother's tropical fish." Craig Dieterly enters the library, leans against a bookshelf, crosses his arms, and smiles at me. Which is even more frightening than when he glares at me. If you've ever seen Jack Nicholson attack Shelley Duvall in *The Shining*, you'll understand what I mean. "You'd better stay away from me," I say, and try to distance myself from Larry Wykoff.

"How come?" Larry Wykoff asks.

"I carry salmonella. It's highly contagious. I might sneeze on you." I'll say anything to get Larry Wykoff to stop talking to me because I would really like to avoid Craig Dieterly turning my life into a world of hurt. "It could be fatal. You never know."

"I really like your delivery," he says. "Who's your favorite stand-up comic?"

"My mother," I answer. I am too distraught to think straight. "Please go. I'm about to eat raw eels. I don't want witnesses."

"You're like a cross between Lenny Bruce and Robin Williams," Larry Wykoff says. "Very dark. Very edgy. Very free-form. Don't you think so, Craig?"

"I sure do, Lair," Craig Dieterly says. "I told him at lunch today just how much I enjoy his special brand of humor. Didn't I, Charlie?"

"Yes," I reply, shifting nervously from one flipper to the other. "You certainly did."

"We'd better get out of here, honey; I promised Amy I'd help her do her nails." Rachel drags Larry Wykoff out the door, leaving me and Craig Dieterly alone in the room.

"I thought I told you to stay away from Banditoes and One-Upsters, Turtle Breath," Craig hisses as soon as the door closes. He takes a step closer to me.

"I tried," I say meekly. "They wouldn't stay away from *me*." I take a step backward.

"You think just because you're suddenly taller than a goalpost you don't have to listen to everything I say?"

"No."

"I can't hear you," Craig taunts, taking another step closer.

"**NO!**" I shout. I try to back up and can't because I have hit the wall and have nowhere to go.

"That's better. Now give me your backpack." Craig Dieterly takes another step toward me and holds his hand out. He is so close I can feel his breath on my neck.

"Oh, come on, Dieterly, my parents gave it to me for my birthday. What are you going to do with it, anyway?"

"Duh . . . make you buy it back from me, Stinky Fish Boy." Craig Dieterly reaches over and snatches it out of my claws with his big stupid hands. "What'll you give me for it?" He dangles it in front of me.

"Uh . . ." I try to think of what I have that Craig might want. "I'll give you one week's allowance if you return it in good condition and promise to leave me alone for the rest of the week."

"Two weeks' allowance and it's a deal," Craig Dieterly says. "But you can forget about the 'leaving you alone' part."

"Oh all right." I sigh. I reach into my pocket and pull out two crisp new five-dollar bills. It's useless arguing with him. Craig Dieterly grabs the money out of my claws and turns to leave.

"Hey, wait!" I protest. "Give me my backpack, Dieterly. We had a deal."

"I'll give it back when I'm good and ready," Craig Dieterly says. "Next time I catch you hanging out with my friends you're not getting off so easy." He doesn't even bother to look at me as he slams the door in my face.

I am so mad I feel like reporting him to Principal Muchnick and getting him put on detention for the rest of his life. Except last week when I reported Craig Dieterly for dropping water bombs on me, Principal Muchnick told me I was acting like a big baby and it was high time I grew up and learned to fight my own battles.

The bell for the end of seventh period rings. I hurry upstairs to Mr. Arkady's office in the science department and give the door a few quick raps with my claw. "Come in, Mr. Drinkvater," Mr. Arkady says. "I am expectink you. Door is open."

The tidy little room has cheery yellow curtains on the window. The bookshelves are filled with skeletons of lizards and frogs and bats and a few carefully preserved tarantulas in glass jars. The occasional freeze-dried snake is artfully arranged as if were about to pounce on its victim. Mr. Arkady sits at his desk humming and fondling a replica of a human skull. He gestures for me to sit down on my crate.

"You have transformed into my favorite extinct animal, Mr. Drinkvater. Congratulations! I luff dinosaurs. They are so resourceful. And powerful. I hope you vill learn to enjoy your new body. Remember: sudden change can be frightenink. But also excitink." He puts down the skull. He studies me closely. "You look like a cross betveen a Diplodocus and an Apatosaurus vit a little salamander thrown in for good measure."

"My grandmother came from a long line of mutant dinosaurs."

"Very interestink, Drinkvater. Your ancestors evolved durink the Devonian period, as you know. Many of your relatives ver viped out durink the Permian-Triassic extinction. My deepest sympathies to your femily, Drinkvater."

"Thanks, Mr. Arkady," I reply. "But wasn't there something else you wanted to say to me? Something important?"

"I vas so excited to see you I almost forgot. I haff two pices of advice for you, Drinkvater," Mr. Arkady begins. "First: you must be the subject of your science report. You vill get high marks for originality, I promise. And you vill discover many vunderful and amazink tinks about yourself along the vay."

What I think is: *What's so wonderful and amazing about turning into a big, smelly lizard?* What I say is: "Good advice, sir."

And then Mr. Arkady stares at me so hard it's like his eyes are boring a hole through me, and for a second I wonder if he is going to bite me in my incredibly long neck and turn me into an undead mutant dinosaur.

"Second: alvays keep your eyes out for udders of your kind as you travel through life or you vill be vun lonely little mutant dinosaur."

"What are you trying to tell me, Mr. Arkady?"

"I am tryink to tell you many thinks, Mr. Drink-vater. But like all good titchers sometimes I don't giff my students the answers. I giff them the qvestions."

Mr. Arkady prefers the Socratic method of teaching. That means that he doesn't give information to his students. He draws it out of them. Now he gets up from his desk and swoops over to me. He raises his eyebrows and stands so close that I can feel his oddly cool breath on my scales.

"The important qvestion of today is: vat do you really know about your family, young man? If you learn more about vair you come from, you vill learn more about vair you are goink."

"I really *would* like to know more about where I'm going, Mr. Arkady," I say. "Only how am I supposed to learn more about where I came from?"

Before he can answer my question, the bell rings and he shoos me away. "School is over for the day. Get goink, Mr. Drinkvater! Hurry before I giff you more homevurk."

I know he is trying to tell me something very important. But what?

12
PICTURE THIS

"**YOU'VE GOT TO** stop letting Craig Dieterly walk all over you, pal," Sam says. "He's out of control." Sam, Lucille, and I are on our way to the bus stop. We are going to my house this afternoon to eat Halloween cookies, carve our pumpkin, and do homework together. I have just explained to my friends why I'm not wearing my backpack.

"It's so unfair. What did you ever do to him?" Lucille asks. "At some point you're going to have to learn to face your fear of Craig Dieterly and just, you know, deal with it."

"I know, I know," I say. "It's right up there at the top of my list of things to do right after 'flap my wings and fly to the moon.'"

"Anyway, what did Mr. Arkady have to say?" Lucille asks.

"I'm not sure," I reply. "But I'll tell you this: he knows something and he's not telling me. I think he wants me to guess. It's pretty frustrating."

"Typical Arkady," Sam says.

The wind whips up the leaves around us as we walk. The sky is an ominous, dull gray. It looks like it's going to start to pour any minute. A perfect afternoon to have your favorite backpack stolen by the person you hate most in the entire world.

As we arrive at the bus stop, I put down my crate for a second and reach for my all-semester student pass—and suddenly realize it's in my backpack. Mrs. Denby, the driver on our route, is so strict she wouldn't let her own mother get on board without one of those things.

"You guys wait here," I say. "The bus'll come any second. I'll hurry on ahead and meet you at my house. My mom will let you in if you get there before me."

"What are you talking about?" Lucille exclaims. "We're not letting you walk home alone from your first day back at school as a creature. Who do you think we are, One-Upsters or something?"

"Yeah. Or Banditoes?" Sam chimes in. "We're Mainframes all the way, and we stick together. If you prick us do we not bleed? If you tickle us do we not laugh? If you poison us do we not keel over and croak?"

We give each other the official Mainframe handshake. I have to be extremely careful not to injure anybody with my claws as we slap our palms together twice, wiggle our shoulders, twirl around, and shout our Mainframe motto, "All for one and one for all." I get so tangled up in my tail I nearly fall flat on my large mutant dinosaur butt.

I wouldn't trade in my Mainframe friends for three million One-Upsters and Banditoes, but as we do our handshake I can't help thinking how much I enjoyed talking to Larry Wykoff. And how surprised I was to discover the good side of Amy Armstrong. Sometimes I wish Lucille and Sam would give the cool kids a break. It's not their fault they're cool. They were born that way.

When we get to my house, Mom opens the door to let us in. "How was your reentry assembly, Charlie?" she asks.

"Charlie rocked, Mrs. D.," Sam answers.

"That's wonderful!" Mom exclaims.

"I did okay," I say.

"He's just being modest, Mrs. Drinkwater. He was seriously funny," Lucille says. "You would have been proud of him."

"I'm always proud of him," Mom says. "Finish hanging up your coats, everybody, and come on in. Mr. Drinkwater is upstairs getting out of his suit, and the pumpkin is sitting on the table just begging to be carved. I hope you brought your appetites. I've got a fresh batch of 'witches on broomsticks' flying out of the oven any second."

"That's great, Mrs. Drinkwater," Lucille says. "It's not officially Halloween until I eat at least five of those things."

"Make that ten," Sam says. "And boy do they smell delicious." We all follow our noses into the kitchen. I try not to drool on the rug.

"Where's Dave?" I ask. We all sit down at the kitchen table.

"He went over to Janie's house, honey." Mom brings over a plate of her famous cookies. "Careful, they're hot." We all take one. "Who wants milk?"

"That's not like Dave," I say, picking off chocolate sprinkles from mine with the tip of my enormous tongue. "He always helps us carve the pumpkin. It's a tradition. Do you think he's still mad at me for trying to eat his fish?"

"Of course not, sweetie. Your brother's just getting a little old for carving pumpkins," Mom says. "Don't you think? And anyway, with the big game only two days away he's got to be really careful with his wrist. It's still pretty sore."

"These witch on a broomstick cookies are even better than last year, Mrs. Drinkwater," Lucille says, licking the crumbs off her lips. "What's your secret?"

"You added a little 'eye of newt' to your cauldron when you stirred the batter, didn't you, Mrs. D.?" Sam polishes off a cookie and reaches for another.

"I sure did. How'd you ever guess, Sam?" Mom says. "And just a pinch of 'toe of frog.' Works like a charm." The front doorbell rings. "I wonder who that could be?" Mom asks, wiping her hands on her apron. She hurries out of the room to get the door. Balthazar wanders in and sniffs around to check the floor for crumbs. He looks at me suspiciously and then trots back to his favorite hiding place behind the living room couch next to the radiator. "Hang up your coat and c'mon in, Janie." I can hear Mom from the other room.

Why is Janie here? I thought Dave just went to her house.

"I'm dying to see Charlie. Everyone in upper school is talking about him. Do you think he'd mind?" Janie Belzer whispers urgently to my mom.

"Not at all, Janie," Mom says. "Follow me. We're about to start carving the pumpkin."

Janie enters the kitchen and stares at me. "Wow," she says softly.

"Sit down and enjoy yourself," Mom says, pulling up an extra chair.

"I think I'll just stand over here for now and watch, Mrs. Drinkwater," she says, hovering between the table and the kitchen counter. I can't tell if she's scared or just excited to see me. She can't take her eyes off me. It's making me pretty self-conscious. Usually Janie Belzer doesn't even notice me. None of Dave's girlfriends does. I'm the invisible little brother. Or at least I was.

"Suit yourself, honey," Mom replies. She lays out spoons for scooping and a set of special pumpkin-carving knives. Sam selects one and carefully carves a jagged line around the top of the pumpkin. When he's done Lucille slowly lifts it off by the stem and rests it on the table. I reach in and scoop out pumpkin seeds with my claws. Janie pulls out a small sketch pad from her bag as I start carefully poking out two big triangles in the pumpkin for eyes.

"Do you think Charlie would mind if I sketched him while he carves the pumpkin, Mrs. Drinkwater?"

"Do us all a favor and don't ask him for his autograph, okay?" Sam groans. He reaches for another cookie. "He already thinks he pretty hot stuff."

"I do not," I protest.

"Why don't you ask him yourself, Janie?" Mom says, pouring milk into frosty mugs for everyone. "He doesn't bite. Do you, Charlie?"

"Don't say stuff like that, Mom," I mutter. "It's embarrassing."

"Would it be okay if I sketched you, Charlie?" Janie asks.

"Yeah. Sure. I guess," I say.

Janie watches me intently as her charcoal pencil flies across the paper. She is making me so nervous that my claw slips as I cut out the big smiling mouth on the pumpkin, and I almost cut myself.

"Look at that, Mrs. D.," Sam says. "Charlie doesn't even need a knife."

"I'm home!" Dave hollers as he opens the front door. "Where is everybody?"

"We're in the kitchen carving the pumpkin, sweetie," Mom calls back. "There's a cookie in here with your name on it. Come and get it while it's hot."

Dave hurries into the room. When he sees Janie sketching me, he stops dead in his tracks. "I just went to your house to pick you up," he says to her after an awkward silence. "What's going on? I thought we were going out for pizza." He doesn't look happy.

"I came here instead," Janie says, squinting at me and holding up her pencil. "We can go out for pizza later. It's not a big deal."

"What're you doing?" he asks.

"I'm sketching your little brother, silly," Janie says. "What's it look like I'm doing?"

"I thought you just did portraits of dogs," Dave says.

"I draw what interests me." Janie shrugs. "I'm interested in lots of things."

"How come you never drew my portrait?" Dave says.

"I don't know," Janie answers.

"Aren't I interesting?" Dave asks as Mom offers him

a cookie. "Not now, Mom, okay?" Dave says. "I'm really not in the mood."

Lucille and Sam and I look around nervously. You can feel the tension in the room. Mom goes over to the counter and quietly rolls out some more cookie dough.

"Honestly, Dave, I don't see why you have to be so grouchy," Janie says.

"I'm not being grouchy!" Dave practically shouts. "I'm being inquisitive!" Balthazar trots back in to see what's up. "I'd just really like to know how come you suddenly find my little brother so interesting. That's all."

"I can't help it if I'm interesting." I get up from the table and bring my plate and mug to the sink. "I didn't do it on purpose."

"Guess that's all the drawing for today." Janie puts away her pad and pencil and heads for the coat closet.

"Aw, c'mon, Janie. Don't leave." Dave follows her into the hallway. "We have a date."

"*Had,*" Janie says as she puts on her coat and hurries out the door. "Nice seeing you, Mrs. Drinkwater."

"Now look what you've done, Charlie," Dave mutters.

"I didn't do anything," I reply.

"Hey, slow down! Wait for me!" Dave runs out of the house, yelling at Janie.

I know Mom and Dad said Dave isn't mad at me anymore. But he sure *seems* mad.

Later that night, after Sam, Lucille, and I have finished our homework and they have gone home, I brush my fangs and put on the shiny green satin pajamas my mom has thoughtfully left hanging in the bathroom. I squeeze myself into bed, exhausted, turn on my night-light, and stare at the ceiling.

I can't stop thinking about what Mr. Arkady said. "If you learn more about where you come from, you will learn more about where you are going." Where does he think I'm going? What does he mean?

At this rate I'll never get to sleep. I amuse myself by making dangerous-looking shadow puppets on the ceiling with my claws until Dave finally tiptoes in around eleven.

"Are you awake?" he whispers.

"Yeah," I reply.

"I'm sorry I got so upset before." Dave hangs up his clothes and goes into the bathroom to brush his teeth.

"It's okay."

"No, it isn't. I'm a little jumpy," he says. "About the game and all."

"I bet."

"It'll be different after Thursday . . . the play-offs . . . you know . . ." He gargles and rinses and then comes back in and slips into bed.

"Yeah. How's Janie?" I ask.

"She told me I was acting like an idiot and I told her I was sorry. I think she's planning on forgiving me."

"I wish I didn't try to eat your fish, Dave."

"I know."

"I won't do it again."

"Yeah," Dave says quietly.

"You're still mad at me, aren't you?" I ask.

"I'll get over it eventually," Dave answers.

"I hope so. I was wondering. . . . When a girl tells you you're interesting, what does that mean exactly?"

"Did someone tell you that you were interesting?" Dave asks.

"Yeah. At lunch period. Does that mean she likes you?"

"Who told you that you were interesting?"

"Amy Armstrong," I reply.

"The most popular girl in middle school told you that you were interesting?"

"Yeah. What do you think that means?"

Dave gives a big sigh. "You know exactly what that means." He punches his pillow really hard, puts it over his head, and gets really quiet.

Now what did I do? Big brothers can be so confusing. I was about to ask Dave what he thought Mr. Arkady meant, but now he's way too upset to answer any more questions.

I watch the moon hide behind a big white cloud. I listen to the steady hum of the motor in my brother's fish tank and the bubbles that gurgle as they flow through the aerator. "Do you think you're going to stop being mad at me at any point in the near future, Dave?"

Oh, c'mon. Say something. It's not going to kill you. I wait. But he doesn't reply.

"Night, Dave. Pleasant dreams." I wait some more. Soon he is fast asleep and snoring peacefully. And I am not.

Notes:

Right on!

An eighth grader noticed me—!! Add four points to my popularity score card.

Today is Herman the Iguana's birthday. Bring dried flies.

sup.

Charlie

Amy A— movie this weekend?

yeah!

Oh, Charlie! I'd love to!!

13

ADD THREE BILLION POINTS
TO MY POPULARITY SCORECARD

"**WELL IF IT** isn't Snow White's other little-known dwarf, Swamp Thing." Craig Dieterly is lying in wait for me on the third-floor landing as I climb the stairs to Mrs. Adams's English class. Second period is about to begin.

"That's so funny I forgot to laugh." I try to make it past him so I can get to the next floor, but he blocks my way. "Let me through, Dieterly, okay?"

"You didn't say please, Drinkwater." He puts his arm up to stop me as I try to go around him.

"Would you *please* let me through, Dieterly?" I am waiting patiently for him to put his arm down when I smell Principal Muchnick approaching. He turns the corner and strides over to see what's going on. He's been following me around all morning.

"Second period starts in approximately—" he looks down and checks his watch—"seventy-five seconds, Drinkwater. I wouldn't be late for any classes if I were in your . . . uhhh . . . flippers. Do I make myself perfectly clear?"

"Yes, sir," I reply.

"And Dieterly, if this character gives you any trouble I expect you to report it to me immediately." Principal Muchnick looks at me sternly. "He's on provisional reentry, in case you didn't already know it."

"Yes, sir," Craig Dieterly replies. "He was being a little disrespectful to me on the stairs just now, but I think I have the situation under control." Craig Dieterly couldn't tell the truth is his life depended on it.

"Watch your step, Drinkwater," Principal Muchnick warns. "The ice upon which you are skating could not get any thinner if it tried. I'm going upstairs now to peruse your psychological evaluation. I trust you can keep your animal instincts in check in the meantime."

"Yes, sir," I say again, looking down at my tail.

The second Principal Muchnick is out of sight Craig Dieterly pulls the little clay vase I made for my parents' anniversary out of his knapsack. It was drying in the arts and crafts room the last time I saw it. "Look what I found, Monstro."

"Give it back, Dieterly. I've been working on that thing forever." But he just smirks and starts tossing it from one hand to the other. "C'mon. You'll break it. Put it down. Please."

Craig Dieterly finally gets tired of throwing my vase around and carries it to the storage room next to the stairs. He walks in and places it on a shelf—right next to my backpack and the missing library book I took out last month.

I was wondering what happened to that book. I should have known.

Craig emerges with a big smile on his face. "Go and get it, it Snaggletooth. This is your lucky day."

"You're up to something, Dieterly. I can tell. What else did you put in there? Sneezing powder?" Last year Craig Dieterly sprinkled that stuff all over my desk and every time I removed one of my books I nearly sneezed my head off.

"I didn't put sneezing powder in there, Drinkwater," he says. "Cross my heart and hope to die."

I do not believe Craig Dieterly for a second. I poke my long neck into the storage room and look around for booby traps. When I don't see any I walk in gingerly, put my vase and my book neatly into my backpack, throw it over my shoulder, and turn to leave.

Something's wrong. This was way too easy.

"Is your middle name Shirley?" Craig Dieterly asks.

"Nope," I say. "Wrong again."

"You think you're so great because you get straight As and score above the ninety-ninth percentile on standardized testing. Well, think again, Beetlejuice. There's more to being smart than just intelligence!" He slams the door tightly shut before I have a chance to even think of escaping. I can hear the lock on the outside of the door click into place and Craig Dieterly chortling.

I'm trapped. I can't afford to be late for Mrs. Adams's English class again. I was late last week when Craig Dieterly buried my Charles Dickens paper under the compost heap out by the soccer field, and I had to go dig it up.

Two "lates" in one month means automatic detention. It's a school rule. And I can't break any school rules because I'm on provisional reentry and Principal Muchnick is dying to suspend me. I could never even *dream* about getting into Harvard with a suspension on my record.

Okay. Think, Drinkwater. You were stupid enough to walk into another one of Craig Dieterly's traps, but you'd sure as heck better find a way to get out of it.

I push against the heavy metal door with all my might. It strains and groans under my weight but refuses to give way. I look around the storage room.

The window. Of course. If I can pry it open, I will squeeze through and creep up the side of the building to the fifth floor where I will slip unnoticed into the back of Mrs. Adams's classroom. We herps are famous for our ability to creep. Ask Mr. Arkady if you don't believe me.

I tug at the window as hard as I can with both claws, but it has been painted shut for so long it won't budge. I try again. And again. At last it starts inching up slowly. And then it flies open the rest of the way with a resounding crash. I stick my neck out and gaze down three floors to the concrete pavement below. Not a tree or a bush or a shrub in sight to break my fall if I slip.

Did I mention that I am terrified of heights?

A wave of nausea is already spreading from my belly up through my neck and into the back of my throat. *C'mon. Pull yourself together, Drinkwater. If King Kong can climb a hundred stories up the Empire State Building with Fay Wray wriggling in his arms, you can creep a couple of floors up Stevenson Middle School with a backpack over your shoulder.*

The bell for second period rings. Okay. Here goes nothing. I'm probably too massive to make it through the window.

I huff and I puff as I try to force my enormous torso through the window. It's like threading a needle with a baseball bat. I get stuck halfway through. I hold on to the window frame with both claws and try to squeeze back in. Nothing moves. I can't go out. I can't go in. I am trapped. I remind myself not to look down. I've got to do something fast before I panic.

Did I mention that I am claustrophobic, too?

I clamp my jaws down on the flagpole that is embedded in the brick wall outside the window and drag myself slowly out the window, leaving a trail of greasy residue along the ledge. Now all I have to do is shinny

fifteen feet up a sheer brick wall without crashing onto the pavement below and turning into a big mutant dinosaur pancake.

I dig one claw into the bricks and plant my other one firmly into the window frame above my head, nearly pulling it out of the wall as I drag myself upward. I manage to get a flipper-hold on the decorative ledge that runs along the fourth floor. If I can stay calm and make it to the fifth floor in one piece, there is a small chance I can get to Mrs. Adams's class before she reports me for being late.

It is then that I notice Dr. Craverly staring at me. He sits at his desk in front of the window that I am clinging to. His mouth is open wide in a frozen, silent mask of terror. Principal Muchnick, Mr. Arkady, and Miss Benson, my social studies teacher, all sit at his side going over my psychological evaluation. They look up and see me hanging onto the window ledge for dear life. I wonder if climbing on school property is against the rules?

I am so distracted that I lose my grip on the window ledge and start slipping back down the wall. I drag my nails along the bricks in an attempt to slow my descent. Finally, in desperation, I hurl my weight sideways and crash through the fourth-floor window, landing on a pile of splintered wood and broken glass at Principal Muchnick's feet. "Don't suspend me, Principal Muchnick," I beg. "I can explain."

Principal Muchnick growls, "You are to stand in the hallway and wait while we discuss your case. Do not move an inch. Understand?"

"Yes, sir." I wait outside the door to Dr. Craverly's office for what feels like hours. When I press my ear to the door I can hear Principal Muchnick telling everyone that I am out of control and that he wants to make an example out of me. Miss Benson agrees. Dr. Craverly talks about my antisocial tendencies and the sharpness of my fangs. Mr. Arkady finally takes the floor.

"Charlie Drinkvater is vun uff the smartest kids in Stevenson Middle School and vun uff the nicest, most decent, most responsible children I have effer known. He has been through a traumatic experience, and he deserves our help and compassion, nut our scorn and fear. Do nut suspend this boy. I am beggink you. Honor him."

I cannot tell you how great it feels to have someone else beside your parents stand up for you when the chips are down.

And then everyone whispers furiously. This goes on for quite a while. At last Mr. Arkady glides from the room, wiping his brow with his crimson red silk handkerchief, and swirling his cape. I have to jump back from the door to avoid getting bashed in the snout.

"You have nut been suspended, Mr. Drinkvater," he explains. "At least for the time beink. But you are on 'final and last vornink.' I'm sorry. It's the best I could do. Stay out uff trouble, please. You are nut a cat. You do nut have nine lifes."

"Thanks, Mr. Arkady."

"Be careful nut to get a svelled head, Mr. Drinkvater. The vun you have is already big enough." Mr. Arkady slinks back up to the science lab, quietly humming the theme to *The Addams Family*, and I make a mad dash for my third period class. I'm not planning to be late for anything ever again if it kills me.

Larry Wykoff and Rachel Klempner hurry by, hand in hand, gazing into each other's eyes. Larry manages to tear away from his beloved long enough to stuff a copy of today's *Sentinel* into the back pocket of my green satin pants. "Check it out," he says. "A beautifully crafted and highly entertaining piece, if I do say so myself. But, then, you give great interview."

"It's just the best newspaper article in the history of newspaper articles," Rachel says. "You are a phenomenon, Charlie Drinkwater. They should name an entire constellation after you. See you later, Mr. Big Deal Celebrity!"

"Great profile, Charlie," Norm Swerling says to me as he runs down the hall. "If you change your mind about going to that movie Saturday night, let me know."

"Way to go, creature guy," Dirk and Dack Schlissel call as they rush by, hurling lateral passes at each other.

Craig Dieterly spots me walking down the hall and looks like he is going to bust a gut. "Next time I lock you into a closet you better stay locked, Smelly Boy," he whispers. "If you think I'm kidding, just try me." He reaches for my backpack, but Mr. Arkady turns the corner just in time, and Craig Dieterly pretends he is wiping some lint off my jacket.

Just as I arrive at class, a number of my fifth-grade fans surround me, blocking the door, and waving their copies of *The Sentinel* in my face. They hold out pens and scream, "Me, me, me!"

"Better get in there now, Charlie," Sam says as he pushes his way through the crowd. "Class is about to begin."

"I've just got to sign a few more of these things," I say. "Hey! Stop pushing or nobody gets an autograph. And I mean it!"

"Leave him be, Sam," Lucille says as she hurries into the classroom. "Pretty soon we'll have to take a number and get in line like everybody else." The final bell sends us all scattering to our seats.

If anyone ever asks to write an article about you for your school paper, say yes. Don't even hesitate. It will immediately add seven points to your popularity scorecard. Add three more if the most popular girl in the middle school and possibly the universe sits down next to you.

"Psst," Amy Armstrong says, poking me in my left flank with a pencil. She has moved her desk so close to mine they're practically touching. Sam and Lucille sit in the row ahead of me. They don't look happy.

Amy Armstrong appears to be handing me a small piece of crumpled paper. I look at her blankly.

"It's a note, silly," Amy whispers. "You take it. You read it. You pass it back with a response. It's not such a big deal."

"Settle down, everyone," Mrs. Adams says. "No whispering in the classroom." And then she starts droning on about Charles Dickens and social reform in the nineteenth century.

A note? Be still, my heart. I take the precious scrap of paper in my claws and hold it tightly, savoring the smell of Amy Armstrong's signature lilac perfume clinging to it. This small but significant act is immediately noted with more than a little interest by Lucille, Sam, and, unfortunately, Craig Dieterly.

I wonder if Amy Armstrong is sending me a note to tell me I have bad halitosis and ask me to breathe in the other direction. I carefully unfold the paper and slowly read it. Then I read it again to make sure I am not hallucinating. This is what the note says:

> To C.D. from A.A.—Having a party at my
> house today after school. B there or B² (square).
> What do you say?

I say HOORAYYYYYYYYYYYYYYYY!!!!! I say I am light-headed at the very thought. *Breathe. Relax. Get a grip, Charlie.* I don't even like Amy Armstrong and her stupid friends. Why would I ever want to belong to their unnecessary and ridiculous clique?

Simple: because I want to be popular so badly I would sell my soul to the devil if I thought it would do any good.

And that is exactly what I am about to do.

Without even thinking, I scribble "Sure" on the bottom of the note and pass it back to Amy Armstrong. And then instantly realize that if Craig Dieterly ever finds out I have set foot into Amy Armstrong's house, my goose will be so cooked you won't be able to scrape it off the bottom of the pot.

I start writing a new note for Amy Armstrong about how I have too much homework to go to her house this afternoon, but letting her know how grateful I am. And asking her for a rain check. I want to be popular. But I also want to survive seventh grade.

Before I have a chance to pass my polite rejection note to her, Amy Armstrong writes something on the little scrap of paper and passes it back to me. "So glad you're coming. Can't wait to see you. It's a secret. Don't tell anyone. Okay?"

"Okay," I write, and quickly pass the note back. The die is cast. At which point both Sam and Lucille pass me their own notes. I open Lucille's: "What does Amy

Armstrong want?" I open Sam's: "What does Amy Armstrong want?"

Uh-oh. I don't know how to reply because (A) it's a secret. (B) if I tell Sam and Lucille, it might hurt their feelings because I was invited and they weren't, and I don't want to be insensitive. And then of course there's always (C) I really, really want to go to Amy Armstrong's house and I am afraid that if I tell Sam and Lucille they will talk me out of going.

So I do what any chicken-livered yellow-bellied coward would do: I lie. "She asked if I would help with her science project and I told her I couldn't. She was pretty upset about it." I write on both notes, and then pass them back. I have "made my own bed," as my father would say, and now I am just going to have to lie in it. No pun intended.

14

GUILT BY ASSOCIATION

SAM, LUCILLE, AND I are sitting together, slurping down the boring Wednesday lunch special at our usual table in the back of the lunchroom. I'm feeling pretty bad about the way I'm treating my two best friends. Correction. I feel like I have a giant neon sign on top of my green scaly head screaming LIAR, LIAR PANTS ON FIRE in big red letters.

"Hey, check it out, guys!" Sam exclaims. "I found an actual piece of beef in my beef stew."

"Uh-oh. Don't look now," Lucille warns. "Guess who's coming over to our table?"

Craig Dieterly approaches, even madder than usual. "Losers like you aren't allowed to pass notes to One-Upsters, Froggy McSlime. Losers like you aren't even allowed to breathe on them. If I ever catch you within ten feet of Amy Armstrong again I will go immediately to Principal Muchnick and tell him you hit me with your tail. And don't think I won't, because if I could get you suspended it would be the happiest day of my life. Understand?"

"Yes," I say meekly as Amy Armstrong glides by, carrying her tray. She nods sweetly at Craig Dieterly, winks at me (I really wish she wouldn't do that), and then goes to sit next to Rachel Klempner at the One-Upsters' table. Craig Dieterly scoops up a fingerful of mashed turnips and flicks them into my face.

"Why are you always picking on Charlie?" Sam asks. I dip my napkin in water and wipe myself off. "What did he ever do to you, Dieterly?"

"He got born. That was enough," Craig Dieterly says, and skulks away.

"It's funny," Lucille observes, sipping a spoonful of her meat-free beef stew, "Amy Armstrong doesn't seem very upset about you not helping her with her science project."

"Yeah," Sam adds, wiping his chin. "I was thinking the same thing."

"She probably doesn't even remember she asked me in the first place. You know how popular people are. I bet she's already got five other people lining up to help her with it." Once you get started with this lying business, it's really hard to stop.

"Probably," Sam says. He doesn't look very convinced. Neither does Lucille.

For the rest of the day I try to avoid seeing (A) Amy Armstrong because Craig Dieterly will kill me if he catches us together. (B) Sam and Lucille because I still haven't come up with a good excuse for not walking home with them after school this afternoon, and at some point the subject is bound to come up. And (C) Craig Dieterly. Because I feel like living to see thirteen.

While I wait for the end-of-the-day bell to ring, I sit quietly in language lab, listening to new vocab words on my earphones and wondering what happens if Amy Armstrong serves rare or unusual food at her party and I can't figure out what utensil to pick it up with. Or if I spill something on the rug. Or blank on somebody's name. What if somebody asks me a difficult sports question? What if there is dancing? What if . . . please, God, don't let this happen . . . we have to play volleyball? Or Ping-Pong?

When the bell finally rings I grab my books and hurry out of the building, hoping I don't run into anybody I don't want to run into.

"Where are you going?" Sam and Lucille are standing right outside. If I were trying to run into them I couldn't have planned it any better.

"Want to walk home with us?" Lucille asks.

"I wish I could. My mom's picking me up today in her truck. She's taking me to the dentist. I've got a cavity in my front left fang. It kills."

"We'll wait with you, pal," Sam says.

"She'll be here any minute. I'll be okay."

"Are you sure, Charlie? We really don't mind waiting," Lucille adds. "Is your fang going to be all right?"

"Sure. Don't wait for me. I'll be fine."

"Well . . . okay," Lucille says, as she reluctantly turns to leave. "As long as you're sure you're sure."

"I'm sure."

"You're still coming over later, right?" Sam says.

"What?" I ask. I'm not paying attention. I'm too

worried I won't get to Amy Armstrong's house on time.

"You didn't forget, did you?" Lucille asks. "It's Wednesday, Charlie. Remember? Wednesday?"

"Of course I remember." Sam and Lucille and I have watched a movie and had dinner together every Wednesday night for the last ten billion years. "I'll meet you guys at Sam's later," I say. "If the dentist says it's okay to go out after my procedure."

"You don't look so hot, Charlie," Lucille says. My two friends shake their heads and leave.

I stay put until they are well out of sight, and then wait around for an extra couple of minutes, in case they change their minds and come back to see how I'm doing and catch me leaving for Amy Armstrong's house. Because my left front fang feels perfectly fine. My mother isn't really coming to pick me up in her truck to take me to the dentist. And I am nothing but a big, fat liar. I call home and tell the answering machine I'm going to a party at Amy's after school.

I am sick to my stomach with guilt. But when I think about how much I have always wanted to get invited to Amy Armstrong's house, and how now that I'm more than five feet four inches tall I'm finally potential Bandito material, the guilt lets up a little and I head for the party.

Before I know it I have walked the ten long blocks to Amy Armstrong's house, and I find myself standing in front of a shiny blue door with the number 16 on it in brass letters. I shift from one flipper to the other and try to remain calm. I feel the traditional "what if I can't think of anything to say" anxiety bubble rising in my chest, so I take out my social security factoid cards and quickly review them for interesting and informative talking points.

"Cow gives birth to two-headed offspring at Schwenks' Dairy Farm Tuesday"—that's not going to fly. "Mixed-use container recycling center opens behind the railroad station in Southern Decatur"—I don't think so. I quickly retire the cards to my back pocket and decide to concentrate instead on telling the joke Dad told last week at breakfast about the Three Wise Men and the camel with the bladder control problem. It's pretty funny. I just hope I can remember the punch line.

Feeling somewhat less anxious, I ring the bell. I always imagined Amy Armstrong's doorbell would sound like enchanted fairies playing on harps or flutes or something. But it just goes *briiing*, like everybody else's doorbell.

No one answers. It's awfully quiet in there. Did I get the day wrong? Wait a minute. I think I hear someone.

As I press my earflaps to the door it suddenly flies open and I stumble into the room, nearly falling into the arms of Mrs. Armstrong, who stands there, horrified, looking like she can't decide whether to scream or run in the other direction.

"You . . . you . . . you must be . . . Charlie," Mrs. Armstrong pants. She seems so scared that she can hardly breathe. "I'm . . . Amy's mom. I've heard . . . so much . . . about you."

I know just what you've heard about me, Mrs. Armstrong. I'm surprised you're not calling the police on your jewel-encrusted cell phone right now. Or animal control.

She takes a deep breath and then bravely holds out her hand to shake mine. I hold out my razor-sharp three-pronged slimy claw in return. She quickly reconsiders and tucks her hand into her skirt pocket. We stand there and stare at each other. I am so uncomfortable I nearly tell my dad's Three Wise Men joke before Mrs. Armstrong breaks the silence. "What are you planning to be for Halloween, young man?" she asks.

"A human," I reply.

"Oh," she says. And the conversation grinds to halt

again, as Mrs. Armstrong's gaze travels to my tail and remains there, transfixed. She bites her lip. She shakes her head. She sighs. "The party's in the den," she says finally, pointing to the door at the end of the living room. "Everybody's waiting for you. If you need anything, let me know. I'll be upstairs." She disappears quicker than you can say "mutant dinosaurs in my living room give me the creeps."

I walk slowly through the living room, careful not to bump into the expensive-looking gold urn sitting precariously on the dainty pedestal next to the couch. Or the collection of finely carved Japanese figurines lined up in neat rows on the coffee table. It's like "the museum of things you could break with your tail" in here.

I look around the room and try to memorize every lamp. Every candy dish. Every picture on the wall. I cannot believe I'm in the actual place where Amy Armstrong opens her Christmas presents. And has her amazing birthday parties. Whoa. There's the piano she practiced on when she rehearsed for the award-winning lower-school production of *Cats*. The sheet music for "Memory" is still resting on it.

I approach the legendary den I have been wanting to see ever since Amy Armstrong's Valentine's Day party back in second grade. I didn't get invited. Neither did Sam and Lucille. The people who *were* invited weren't supposed to talk about it. Guess what? They did. Dirk and Dack Schlissel told everyone there was a flat-screen high-def TV in there with surround sound and three-dimensional capabilities. Plus a soda fountain with icy-cold root beer on tap. And seventeen flavors of ice cream. Rachel Klempner told Alice Pincus, who told Sam, that there was a Ms. Pacman game and a professional karaoke machine in there, too. But I think the rumors about the indoor lap pool were just that. Rumors.

A little sign hangs over the doorknob. It says BEWARE: PARTY ANIMALS INSIDE. I decide to take my chances. I smooth down the rumples in my green satin shirt, check out my fangs for signs of stray spinach, remind myself to breathe deeply, and open the door.

15

WHAT'S A NICE MUTANT DINOSAUR LIKE ME DOING IN A PLACE LIKE THIS?

AMY ARMSTRONG'S DEN is not at all the way I imagined. After my eyes adjust to the flickering light from the old lava lamp on the coffee table, I notice a couple of Banditoes sitting on a worn-out sofa with One-Upsters at their side, munching on corn chips, sipping cans of diet soda, and looking bored. I wander farther into the room. The Black Eyed Peas blare from somebody's iPod mini-deck.

I don't see any soda fountains. Just a couch and a couple of chairs and tables in front of a plain old regular

Samsung television set. No 3-D capabilities. Not an external speaker in sight. Rachel Klempner and Larry Wykoff lie on the floor in front of it, holding hands as usual and watching a *Seinfeld* rerun.

Oh no. He's here. I spot Craig Dieterly on the far side of the room. I quickly turn to leave. It's dark. I'm green. The room is crowded. Maybe he doesn't see me.

"What took you so long?" Amy Armstrong asks, re-applying her lip gloss.

"I had to stay late to clean my desk," I reply.

"Go try some of my mom's guac. It's rad. She puts fresh cilantro in it. And anchovies. Aren't they like your distant cousins or something?" Amy Armstrong winks at me and then takes out a pocket mirror and looks lovingly at herself.

I head for the coffee table, grateful for any excuse to get away from her. Craig Dieterly is watching. Staring, actually. Make that glaring. I nearly get knocked over by the Schlissel twins, who are playing a rousing game of "catch the potato chip without using your hands." A couple of cheerleaders egg them on with an occasional, "catch the chip, catch the chip, rah rah rah, in your mouth, in your mouth, sis boom bah."

"Hey, creature guy, catch this!" Dack Schlissel yells as he tosses a few potato chips in my direction. My enormous tongue zaps those chips practically before they leave his hand.

"Way to go!" Dirk Schlissel shouts. "Fastest mouth in the West!" He throws me a few more.

I stand by myself in the corner and wait patiently for the party to start. Everyone mills around, watches TV, talks, and eats potato chips. After a while it dawns on me that this *is* the party.

Craig Dieterly sidles over to me. "You think I can't do anything to you because Amy Armstrong's watching and all of a sudden you're on her good side. But I'm not finished with you, Godzilla. I've got a great big surprise planned for you, and here's a hint—you're going to hate it." He lowers his voice and whispers, "It's Rumpelstiltskin, isn't it?"

"You're not even close." I back away from him. He sticks out his foot to trip me and sends me crashing to the floor. "Don't say I didn't warn you," he says quietly.

I land right next to Larry Wykoff, narrowly missing his head. I can see the headline now: "Creature Nearly Squishes Successful Journalist at Shindig."

"Get me another diet soda, will you, sweetie-kins?" Rachel Klempner asks.

"Sure thing, Rache," Larry Wykoff says, and gets up.

"Love you, mean it," Rachel Klempner says.

"Me too," Larry Wykoff answers.

"You have to say it out loud, Lair, or it doesn't count," she pouts.

"Yeah, but everybody's watching, Rache," he says under his breath. "It's embarrassing." Rachel Klempner glares at him like she might kill him any second. Craig Dieterly watches like a hawk. "Okay. Love you, mean it," he finally says, and she gets this big smile on her face. There's a lot of stuff about this dating business I will never understand.

"C'mon," he tells me. I am happy to follow Larry Wykoff away from Craig Dieterly and into the kitchen, where Mrs. Armstrong keeps the refreshments. "Rache really gets to me, sometimes," Larry Wykoff says, opening the fridge and rummaging around for a fresh can of diet soda. "She has an awesome sense of humor. And she's fun to hang with. And she's sooo cute. But sometimes she gets so bossy I just want to run and hide. Did you ever go out with anybody like that?"

"Sure," I lie. I'm not about to admit that I have never even held a girl's hand except my mother's. "Technically speaking, I'm not seriously involved with her at the moment. But things got pretty intense last summer between me and this girl I know from day camp."

The only thing that was intense between me and Jessica Goldfrank was how much she didn't like me. Right about now is when my nose would start growing like Pinocchio's. If I had a nose.

"Jessica had two entirely different personalities. Good Jessica was kind and helpful. Bad Jessica was like a drill sergeant in the marines. Did you ever see *Dr. Jekyll and Mr. Hyde*? It happens to be one of my favorite movies. Spencer Tracy was amazing. So was Ingrid Bergman. She was in *Notorious*. I bet you didn't know that." Sometimes when I'm uncomfortable I can't stop talking.

"I think I missed that one," Larry Wykoff says.

"You'd like it. It's about this really nice guy who drinks a magic potion and then turns into a monster and goes around killing people."

"Sounds like Rache after a big piece of chocolate cake." Larry Wykoff laughs. "She makes Rambo look like a wimp."

"Like I said, I'm familiar with the type. Nip it in the bud, Larry. Fast. Stop calling her so much. Don't e-mail her back right away. Make a date and then forget to pick her up. And when you've got her feeling really insecure, flirt with another girl. She'll be treating you like a king in no time. Trust me. I've been there." Once I hop on board the lying train there's no stopping me.

"Thanks for the advice, Charlie," Larry Wykoff says, pouring diet soda into a Styrofoam cup. "We'd better get back to the den now or you-know-who will send out a search party looking for us." We head back to the den. "You have my vote, that's for sure."

"What are you voting for?" I have no idea what he is talking about.

"Bandito, of course," he says. "We're considering new members this week. If Amy likes you, you're a shoo-in. If you get blackballed, she has the power to override. Just don't get a double blackball. Even Amy couldn't help you then. We announce the results on Friday. I think you have a real shot."

What? Me? Bandito???????? Whoa! Pinch me quick to see if I am dreaming.

"My hero," Rachel Klempner coos, as Larry Wykoff

hands her the diet soda and lies back down on the floor beside her.

"No prob, Rache," Larry Wykoff says, winking at me. I wander over to some One-Upsters enjoying a lively game of Go Fish in the corner.

Amy Armstrong walks over and stops me in my tracks.

"You're not like the others, Charlie," she says. "You're so wild. So . . . different. Quick, tell me something interesting and unusual. I'm so tired of the same old small talk I'm about to go into spontaneous hibernation." One-Upsters and Banditoes stop playing cards and look up attentively.

I reach into my pocket and fumble around for my social security blanket cards. I scan them quickly and select one. "Say, here's a little-known interesting and unusual fact, Amy," I announce with as much confidence as I can muster. "A mixed-use container recycling center is scheduled to open behind the railroad station next Tuesday. It's the only mixed-use recycling center within a twenty-mile radius of greater downtown Decatur. I'll bet you didn't know that, did you?"

Instantly the room gets quiet and everyone stares at

me. If somebody doesn't say something pretty soon I will pack up my tent and move to an alternate universe. The wrong factoid can be worse than no factoid at all. Craig Dieterly gloats at me from across the room.

Amy Armstrong finally speaks. "Wow, Charlie Drinkwater. I've got to hand it to you. It takes a lot of guts to say something that strange. You are one bad mutant dinosaur." Everyone mumbles in quiet agreement and looks at me with admiration. Craig Dieterly scowls and turns away.

All of a sudden I fit in. I play "catch the jelly beans with your tongue" with the Schlissel twins. It is the only sport at which I have ever excelled. And then Larry Wykoff, Rachel Klempner, and I discover that we all love *Star Trek*. We compare favorite episodes. Larry and I love the movie where Captain Kirk disappears during the maiden voyage of the *Enterprise-B*, but is recovered from an alternate plane of existence. Rachel prefers the episode where Spock returns to Vulcan to find a mate.

Time flies when you're having fun, and before long it's seven thirty and Amy Armstrong is walking me to the door and thanking me for coming. "I'm so glad you came to my little party," she says. "Did you have fun?"

"Yeah. It was epic," I say. "Thanks."

"You're okay in my book, Charlie Drinkwater." Amy Armstrong opens the door for me.

"Thanks," I say. "So are you."

Amy Armstrong flashes her beautiful smile at me one last time before she shuts the door.

16
TROUBLE IN PARADISE

"YOU SURE LOOK pleased with yourself," Mom says as I dance into the kitchen shaking my tail and humming. "How was the party?" she asks.

"It was fly, Mom," I reply. "Very fly. What happened in here?"

The entire kitchen is littered with cookie sheets, bags of potato starch, half-filled mixing bowls, and empty egg cartons. "I'm testing my gluten-free Asian dumplings for Mrs. Pagliuso's garden party. It's a new recipe. I found it on the Internet. Can you hand me my spatula, sweetie?"

"Sure." I grab the spatula, steal a dumpling, and pop it into my jaws. It is as hard as concrete and tastes like rocks. Mom pops a batch into the oven.

"Your brother's still at practice. The big game's tomorrow. I don't know where he finds the energy. Oh, by the way, Sam called. He wanted to know if you were all right. He said he and Lucille were expecting you at his house this afternoon and you never showed up. He wanted to know how you were." My mom rolls out another sheet of dough.

I nearly choke on my concrete dumpling as I leap up from my crate. "This is terrible. Wednesday night is 'dinner and a movie night' at Sam's house. I've never missed it before in my life. Sam and Lucille reminded me about it this afternoon. What did you tell him?"

"I told him not to worry," Mom answers. "I said you were at a party at Amy Armstrong's and you'd be back around seven thirty." She starts cutting out more of the jawbreakers.

"NOOOOOOOOOOOOO!!!!!!!!!!!!!" I scream. "I was supposed to call him and say the dentist told me to rest my sore fang, and I totally forgot."

"Did I do something wrong?" Mom asks.

"Yes!" I race to the closet. "And boy am I in trouble!"

"Is your fang okay, Charlie?" Mom asks, concerned.

"You wouldn't understand, Mom."

"Where are you going?"

"Sam's house." I grab my cape and fly out the door quicker than you can say "Charlie Drinkwater has cauliflower for brains."

"Back from the dentist so soon?" Sam asks coolly as he opens the door a crack. "Hope your fang is feeling better."

"You're looking really good, Sam," I say. He is dressed in his Humpty Dumpty costume. It looks great on him, since he is already kind of egg-shaped.

"It's not finished. I'm still working on it. What do you want?" Sam replies.

"I came to apologize," I say. "C'mon, Sam. Open the door and let me in. It's getting cold out here."

"I didn't think cold bothered you," Lucille says, poking her head around the door. "I thought you were ectothermic." Lucille has on her meter maid costume. She's been a meter maid for Halloween as long as I can remember. She looks just like her regular self only she wears a gray paper hat that says METER MAID and has a couple of parking tickets pinned to her shirt. Lucille is not really into the costume thing.

"I thought you were a friend." Sam holds up a copy of today's school paper. "Great article. Lucille and I especially liked the part where you talk about what it's like to travel around in a pack of hopeless losers."

I guess I went a little overboard during my interview. I came up with a few good jokes about how unpopular me and my friends were. I told Larry Wykoff that people couldn't avoid us any more if we had bubonic plague. You'd think Sam and Lucille would have known I was only trying to sound funny and cool for my article.

Sam tugs nervously at his nose ring. It pops off and drops into the neck of his costume. He sticks his arm down and feels around for it. Lucille and I pretend we don't notice.

"I was running out of things to say," I reply. "I didn't mean you, personally."

"That's very comforting," Lucille says.

"Look, I'm really sorry. Give me a chance, okay? I can explain." I fidget awkwardly from one flipper to the other.

"What's to explain?" Sam says. "You lied to us and then you blew us off. It's simple. Why don't you go hang out with your new friends? Clearly they're more important to you than we are."

"That's not true," I protest. "Look, I never should have lied to you. But I didn't want to tell you I was going to Amy Armstrong's house because I thought you'd be upset you weren't invited."

"Upset!" Lucille exclaims. "Why would we be upset? We don't *like* Amy Armstrong and her stupid friends. We wouldn't go to her house if she begged us. Who wants to hang out with a bunch of boring and pretentious idiots?"

"They're not boring and pretentious idiots, Lucille," I reply. "They're a lot of fun once you get to know them."

"Why would I want to get to know people I hate?" Lucille asks.

"Listen, hotshot," Sam says, "if you think those meatballs really like you, you're crazy. You're just the new flavor of the month. In about five minutes they'll get used to you and drop you like a hot potato."

"That is so not true! You take that back, Sam Endervelt!" I am practically shouting.

"It is true," Sam answers. "You just don't like hearing it."

"For your information, they're considering me for Bandito," I say. "You're just jealous."

"I have to go work on my eggshell. I can't take any more of this." He digs his nose ring out of his costume, clips it back on his nose, turns on his heels, and leaves.

"I'm taking my apology off the table!" I shout.

"Good. Because we wouldn't have accepted it, anyway," Lucille says. She slams the door in my face.

"Why didn't you tell Sam and Lucille you were going to Amy's in the first place, sweetie?" I'm back in the kitchen with my very large head in my very large claws. Mom takes out a big ceramic mixing bowl and starts to assemble another batch of gluten-free concrete dumplings. "Wouldn't that have made life a whole lot easier?"

"Yeah, but they would have talked me out of going. They're no fun. They never want me to do anything except hang out with them."

"Do you really think it was worth lying about?" Mom asks.

"No. Yes. I don't know. Maybe," I say. "I'm not proud about lying to my friends, Mom. And I feel bad about getting caught. But I'm glad I went to that party. And I really want to be a Bandito. I don't care what Sam and Lucille say. You wouldn't understand, Mom. Nobody does."

"Oh, I think I do," Mom says. "I was a kid once myself, you know." She adds two cups of milk and folds in egg whites, soy sauce, and potato starch.

"I hate when you say stuff like that, Mom."

Mom puts down her measuring cup and wipes some starch off her nose. She comes over to me, reaches up, and tries to put her arm around my shoulders. "It isn't easy being a teenager, Charlie," she says. "It can be scary. And lonely. And confusing. But you'll get through it with flying colors. Trust me. I have faith in you, sweetie."

"I'm glad someone does, because I sure don't."

"You must be starving. C'mon. Pull up your crate and enjoy a big plate of gluten-free Asian dumplings. I made a whole extra batch just for you."

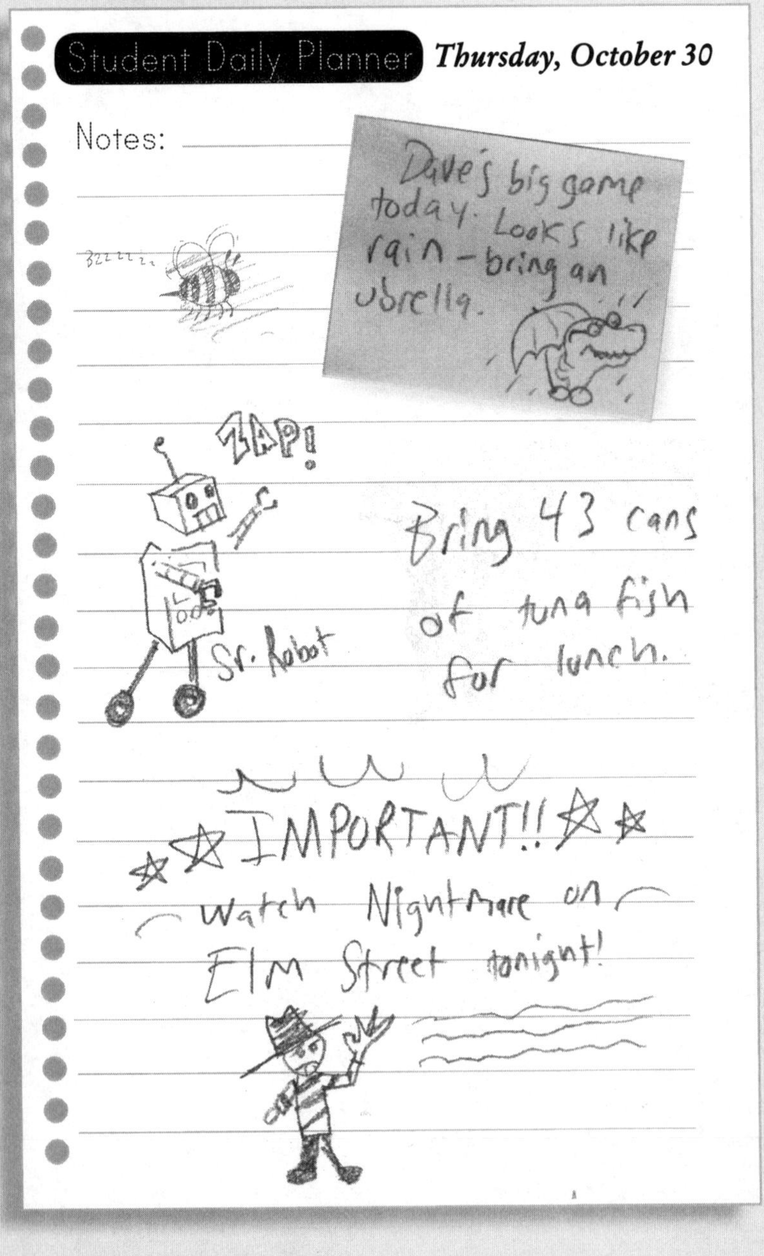
Student Daily Planner
Thursday, October 30
Notes:
Dave's big game today. Looks like rain – bring an ubrella.
ZAP!
Sr. Robot
Bring 43 cans of tuna fish for lunch.
IMPORTANT!!
Watch Nightmare on Elm Street tonight!

17

I SMELL A RAT

BANDITOES AND ONE-UPSTERS are voting today to decide whether I will become socially acceptable at long last, or remain stuck for eternity on the absolute lowest rung of the popularity ladder. Sam and Lucille and I still aren't speaking to each other. Principal Muchnick keeps following me around to make sure I don't break any more rules. And everywhere I go I see Craig Dieterly lurking in the shadows, waiting to spring out and teach me a lesson I will never forget. No wonder my stomach hurts.

"Show me where, Charlie?" Nurse Nancy asks.

"Here." I point to my distended belly. "It kills. I can't stop burping. And I feel like I'm about to throw up." I am sitting on my crate in Nurse Nancy's office feeling sad and lonely and sorry for myself.

"Oh, dear," she says. "You'd better lie down." She motions to the cot in the corner of the room.

"I'll just sit here, if that's okay. I'm a little big for the cot." I couldn't squeeze myself onto three of those things.

Nurse Nancy drags over a large wastebasket and places it beside me. "Just in case," she says. "I'll be right back. Don't move." She puts a cold compress on my forehead and hurries out of the room. It actually does make me feel a little better. Principal Muchnick pokes his head through the door.

"What's up?" he asks. I point to my stomach and moan. "You'd better not be faking again, that's all I can say, Drinkwater. Feigned illness is an official no-no. Section eight, paragraph three in the rule book."

I burp loudly. It smells pretty bad. Principal Muchnick is out of that room faster than you can say "mutant dinosaur burps are disgusting."

Soon Mr. Arkady glides effortlessly into the room,

followed by Nurse Nancy. "You are lookink terrible, Mr. Drinkvater," he says. "Stick out your tunk."

"My what, Mr. Arkady?"

"Tunk," he repeats. "Tunk!" And then he sticks out his tongue and points to it.

"Are you sure, Mr. Arkady?" I ask.

"Don't be shy, Mr. Drinkvater. Vee have all seen tunks before."

I stick out the first few feet. Nurse Nancy turns a sickly yellow and looks like she is going to pass out. Mr. Arkady reaches into his white lab coat and quickly slips on latex examining gloves. He carefully explores the tip of my tongue. "Hmm . . . lean beck, pleace." He palpates my big round stomach. "Does this hurt?"

"A little, sir," I reply.

"Open your mouth and say 'ahh.'" He takes out a little flashlight from his lab coat and peers into my throat. "Very interestink."

"What's wrong with me, Mr. Arkady?" I ask.

"A little acid reflux, maybe, Mr. Drinkvater," he replies. "Nuthink serious."

"Is there anything I can do about it?"

"Sure," he answers. "Eat less. Cut out fatty foods.

And reduce stress leffels. A saltine cracker at bedtime can do vunders." He reaches into his lab coat again and pulls out two white tablets. "Take these. They vill help."

"What are they, Mr. Arkady?" I ask.

"Tums. They cause tremendous farts in chimpanzees and lizards, so vatch out every-buddy." Nurse Nancy runs from the room. Mr. Arkady tosses the tablets into my waiting jaws, takes out a soft cotton pad, and begins rubbing my belly with it.

"Sometimes it is difficult to be a teen-itcher," he says. "The stress of adolescence can be terrible. Alvays tryink to fit in. And feelink socially unacceptable. Phooey. Who needs it? You must relax. And breathe dipply. Every-tink vill be okay. I guarantee it. Please stop vurryink."

"Thanks, Mr. Arkady," I say. "I'm feeling a little bet-ter now." Mr. Arkady really gets what I'm going through.

"That's good."

"But I'm awfully sleepy."

"That's because I am rubbink your belly."

"Are you hypnotizing me, Mr. Arkady?" I ask.

"I hope so, Mr. Drinkvater."

"It's vurking. I mean working," I say, as my eyes be-gin to close and my head slumps to the floor.

"You vill feel much better ven you avaken," he whispers.

After what feels like several seconds I hear the end-of-the-day bell and suddenly awake with a start to realize that I have spent the entire day in Nurse Nancy's office. I hurry downstairs to wait for my parents to pick me up and take me to Dave's big game.

It's cold and damp outside. My favorite kind of weather. One of my fifth-grade fans comes over to me and tugs at my shirt sleeve, holding up a piece of paper for me to autograph.

"How much can you get for one of those things?" I ask. Something funny is going on in my stomach. It feels like a volcano is about to explode down there.

"A quarter," he replies.

My price has dropped substantially since yesterday. The boy doesn't even call me "sir." If I ever get to be a Bandito maybe my price will go up.

As I write, an overpowering urge to pass wind gets the best of me, and I release a torrent of Tums-induced flatulence into the air, accompanied by the loudest fart in the history of farting. It sounds like a hundred whoopee cushions, only louder. Mutant dinosaur burps smell like roses compared to this. The stench is overpowering. My eyes begin to water, and I feel like throwing up again.

"Oh my God, who cut the cheese?" The fifth-grader drops my autograph and staggers off, gagging. "Quick, somebody, hand me a gas mask!" he shouts. "I'm dying here." I fan the air around me with my tail.

A streak of lightning slashes through the sky. There is a loud clap of thunder and the sky opens up. Mom's beat-up pickup truck chugs slowly toward me, huffing and puffing. It backfires loudly and comes to a stop in front of the building. "I thought you'd never get here," I say.

"Hop in!" Dad says. He gets out of the cab and comes around to unlatch the back for me. He holds up a folded newspaper to keep the rain off his shiny bald head. "I left a tarp in there for you," he tells me. "Better get under it. Mom's afraid you'll catch cold."

"I'll be fine," I say, climbing onto the truck bed. "I'm a lizard, remember? I practice thermo-regulation."

"Hurry it up, son. The game starts in ninety minutes and we're already running late. We promised Dave we'd get there for the opening kickoff." Dad slams the tailgate shut behind me.

"It was all my fault," Mom calls from the driver's

seat. "I got stuck behind a parade on the way to pick up your father. Who knew it was Polish Pride Day?"

"We've got to get out of here immediately, Doris," Dad warns. He shakes the rain off himself and gets back into the cab. "There's a powerful smell of methane in the air today."

He quickly rolls up his window, and we lurch out of the driveway. Springfield is forty miles away. They're making repairs on the main highway, so we have to take back roads. The rain is coming down in sheets. Like everything else in this old truck, the windshield wipers don't work very well. I really hope we get there on time. I know how much this game means to my brother.

After about fifteen minutes, Mom puts on the brakes and the old truck grinds to a halt in the middle of the road.

"Looks like some kind of accident up ahead," I say, hopping out of the truck bed. "I'll go over and see what's happening."

"Be careful, sweetie," Mom says. "It's awfully wet out there."

It sure is. I slide through a river of mud as I pass about a dozen stopped cars. I come to a shiny new Ford lying under a giant fallen oak. Its massive trunk and limbs block the road completely. The driver stands outside his car, shaking his head and staring sadly at the hood, which is crumpled like an accordion.

"Are you okay, mister?" I ask.

"That tree just missed me by about six inches. Hate to even think about it," he replies. As he turns to look at me, a flash of lightning illuminates the sky, and I see a look of horror cross his face as he realizes he is talking to a creature. His eyes bulge. The blood drains from his face. "Who are you? *What* are you?"

"I'm Charlie Drinkwater, sir," I say, holding out my claw politely. "I'm in the seventh grade at Stevenson Middle School. Pleased to meet you." Suddenly I let loose with another stink bomb, and the man pulls out a handkerchief and covers his face. Memo to self: Don't take any more Tums. Ever.

"Get away from me, you m-m-m-m-monster!" he stammers. "Heeeelp!!!!!!!!!!"

"Anything I can do, mister?" My father approaches, holding his nose and carrying a small red plastic mug. "Cup of coffee?"

The man grabs the cup and runs to his car. He cowers behind it, covering his nose with his handkerchief.

"We called the police," Dad says. "They say it'll take them half an hour to get here. What with the rain and the mud and all."

"What about the game?" I ask. "Dave will be so disappointed."

"We'll make it there by halftime, son." Dad brushes the rain from his shoulders. "I just hope he understands."

I make a decision. "Stand back," I say.

"What are you going to do, son?" Dad asks.

"You'll see." I head straight for the tree in the middle of the road.

My mom puts up her big yellow umbrella and hurries over to see what I'm doing. "Don't hurt yourself, sweetie!" she yells. She joins my dad and about twenty other drivers and passengers who have gotten out of their cars and come over to look at me and the tree.

"I'm okay, Mom, don't worry!" I yell back. I lean over, dig my claws into the tree, and attempt to drag it away from the middle of the road. My flippers sink into the soggy ground. I take a deep breath. I plant my legs firmly beneath my bulging torso and pull the tree with all my might, but I can't seem to budge it.

I let go and the tree falls back into the mud, splattering me from my flippers to the top of my head. I wipe my hooded eyelids with my claws, wrap my giant tail tightly around the tree, and hold on with all my might. I start walking slowly but surely, dragging the mighty oak with every painful step. The rain beats down on my scales. Every muscle in my body strains from the effort.

No one utters a sound until I have at last deposited the tree safely by the side of the road and collapse beside it, panting. The crowd bursts into a spontaneous round of applause, covering the sound of yet another one of my tremendous farts.

The man with the crushed Ford emerges from behind his car and walks over to us, still clutching the handkerchief to his face. "Wow. That's a very unusual kid you have there," he tells my dad. He gingerly holds out his hand to me. I take it in my claws and shake it gently.

"We like to think so," Dad replies, holding his nose tightly.

"He's only twelve," my mom adds proudly. She leans over and whispers in my ear, "Get into the truck, son. Quickly. I smell a herd of cows approaching."

Everybody heads back to their cars. Soon we are chugging down the road again. I wipe the mud from my body and try to catch my breath. The rain is letting up. I stick my head through the window. "Think we're going to make it, Dad?"

"It sure looks like it," Dad answers, relieved.

We pick up speed, and it is smooth sailing for several minutes—until the truck suddenly lurches violently. The engine sputters and dies. Everything gets very quiet. We coast silently for a few more feet, land right in the middle of a giant mud puddle, and, with a sickening gurgle, sink several feet into the ooze.

I stay in the broken-down truck with Mom while Dad hitches a ride into town, rents a U-Haul van, and comes back to get us. It takes forever. We drive the rest of the way to Springfield in near silence. "It doesn't look good, does it?" I ask. Dad just stares at his watch and sighs.

18
WINNING ISN'T EVERYTHING

WE GET TO the big game just as Dave completes a thirty-seven-yard pass into the end zone that breaks the tie with the Springfield Sprinters and clinches the play-offs for the Stevenson Salamanders. Ecstatic fans wearing big rubber salamander hats are screaming their heads off as we watch Dave's teammates carry him away on their shoulders, chanting, "We love Dave! We love Dave!" over and over.

My brother breaks into a huge grin when he sees us coming.

"I'm MVP, Dad! Can you believe it, guys?" Dave yells.

"That's great, son!" Dad yells back. "Congratulations!" I haven't seen Dave this happy for a long time.

When things finally calm down, Dad tells Dave that not only did we miss the opening kickoff, we were so late we missed the entire game. Dave is so disappointed he looks like he is going to cry. "All I wanted was for you guys to come and watch me play the most important game of my life," he says. "Was that too much to ask? One lousy game?" We go back to the rented U-Haul van and wait in silence while Dave showers and changes into his regular clothes.

At last Dave gets into the van and we start the long ride home. "If you really wanted to see me play, you never should have taken that old junk heap in the first place, Mom. It's always breaking down and you know it." Dave's voice cracks when he speaks.

"We really wanted to get to the game on time, honey, but we had to take the truck," Mom explains. "Charlie's way too big to fit into a regular car."

"It's all about Charlie again," Dave says flatly.

"Don't blame me. It's not my fault," I protest. "I

didn't *ask* to be an oversized creature who can't fit into cars, Dave. You're just upset 'cause you're used being the only one in the family who gets any attention."

"Yeah. Right," Dave says. "Like I care. Believe me, if I wanted to be jealous of anybody, Charlie, it wouldn't be you."

"I didn't say you were jealous of me, Dave," I protest loudly. "That's not at all what I'm talking about. You never understand me."

"Then why the heck don't you say what you mean!" Dave shouts.

"Children, stop it this minute," Dad orders sternly. "Charlie, don't be so argumentative. Dave, don't yell at your little brother. It's not nice."

After several minutes, Mom breaks the silence. "If we didn't take the truck tonight we would have had to leave Charlie at home. And I know you wouldn't have wanted that, Dave."

"Would that have been so terrible?" Dave asks. "Charlie doesn't even *like* football. He doesn't know the first thing about it. He could have stayed home and written another one of his A papers like he always does. He wouldn't have cared. Why does everybody worry about

Charlie all the time? Why doesn't anybody ever worry about me for a change?"

"I *do* worry about you, Dave," I tell my brother. "And no matter what you say, we really tried to get to your game on time, and I'm totally sorry we didn't make it."

"Apology not accepted," Dave grumbles.

"Don't be so stubborn, honey," Mom says. "We all worry about you, Dave."

"We're proud of you, son," Dad says quietly. "We know you worked like a dog to win that award tonight. And we wish we could have witnessed your great success. But it wasn't your mom's fault we didn't get there. And don't blame Charlie, either. This afternoon your little brother carried a giant oak tree all the way across a rain-soaked street so that we could get to that game on time. I just want you to know that."

"I don't care. I still feel terrible." Dave's voice drifts off and he stares out the window. "I want to crawl into bed and pretend tonight never happened."

Just because your big brother is older than you, it doesn't always mean he's more grown up.

Balthazar is the only one who seems the least

bit interested in food tonight. He barks happily when he hears everyone coming and sniffs for signs of hidden surprises in our pockets as we hang up our rain-soaked coats. He doesn't seem afraid of me anymore. I'd say "wary" is more like it. It's not much. But it's an improvement.

"Aren't you going to Janie's house, Dave?" Mom asks. "I thought she was having everybody over for the after-party."

"She is," Dave replies. "I told her I had to go home and soak my wrist."

"Did you hurt yourself again?" I ask.

"No," he replies tersely. "I don't exactly feel like celebrating tonight."

When we get up to our room Dave puts his MVP trophy on his bookshelf next to his eight million other trophies and then gets ready for bed. I pull my crate over to my desk and start doing my math assignment: "Car X and Car Y leave Chicago at exactly the same time. Car X travels at an average speed of forty-two miles per hour. Car Y travels . . ." I hear the click of Balthazar's nails in the hallway. I look up and see him hovering in the doorway, watching me cautiously.

"Hey, Bally. What's up?" I ask. He whines softly. "Don't be afraid, boy." I crane my long, skinny neck over and lean my head way down so I am eye to eye with him. "Want a treat?" His ears perk up, and I can tell he is listening to me really hard. A glimmer of recognition crosses his big brown eyes. He barks softly and wags his tail. I think he has just figured out who I am.

"It's me. Charlie," I whisper. "It's really me." I take the liver snap out of my pocket. I have been carrying it around with me all week, waiting for just the right moment to give it to him. I hold it out in my claws. He cocks his head to one side and stares at me.

"Take it. Go on. I won't hurt you, Bally. I want us to be friends again." He walks slowly over to the bed and takes the liver snap from my claw in his lips. "Good Bally." His tail thumps loudly on the floor. "I've really missed you, pal."

"Who are you talking to?" Dave asks me as he comes out of the bathroom and gets into bed.

"Nobody."

"Oh. For a second I thought you were talking to me."

"I wasn't."

"That's good," Dave says. "Because I don't much feel

like talking to anybody tonight." He switches off the light beside his bed, punches his pillow a couple of times, and then tosses and turns. I listen to the whistle of a far-away train. In a few minutes I can hear my brother softly snoring.

I look over at Balthazar. He hasn't taken his eyes off me. He waits near the head of my bed and tentatively holds out his paw. I reach out slowly and take it in my claw. I don't want to frighten him. "Come up here with me, Bally," I whisper. "C'mon. You can do it. Up, boy." I pat the covers next to me. "Up."

For a few long moments Balthazar looks at me like he is trying to make up his mind, and then he leaps onto my bed, turns around twice, and snuggles up right next to me. "Good boy." He has, it appears, made peace with my transformation at last. I'm glad to know that at least somebody has.

Student Daily Planner
Friday, October 31
Notes:
Write essay on "Mutant Dinosaurs I Have Known" for science class.
Stay away from Amy Armstrong.
Die, charlie!
She WANTS to KILL me.
BOO!
city scape
meow

19
TRICK OR TREAT

FOUR SLEEPY DRINKWATERS sit quietly around the kitchen table playing with our food. We're still recovering from last night. "Who wants more scrambled eggs?" Mom asks. Dead silence. "Well, don't everybody answer all at once." She shuffles over to the stove to pour herself another cup of coffee. My stomach is feeling better today. But that's about it for good news on the home front.

Dave chugs the rest of his orange juice, and when he gets up from the table, Dad stops him. "Where are you headed, son?" he asks.

"I have to pick up Melanie Lindstrom, Dad." Girl-friend number two—rock climbing, snow globes, and a ponytail, in case you didn't remember. "I walk her to school every Friday. You know that."

"Mind if I walk with you to Melanie's, Dave?" Dad asks.

"I'm not really in the mood for company, Dad," he replies.

"It wasn't really a question, son," Dad says. "I'm walking with you to Melanie's. It's about time you and I had a little chat." Dad puts his arm around Dave's shoulder and they head for the kitchen door. Dad looks over meaningfully at Mom, who just sighs and clears the breakfast dishes.

"Oh great," Dave says, and slams the kitchen door behind them.

I was beginning to think that I was the only one in the family who had to have family chats.

I go upstairs and lay out my human costume: one of Dad's beat-up hats, the polka-dot tie Aunt Harriet gave Dave for his last birthday, and an old briefcase I found at the bottom of the front hall closet.

I put the hat on top of my pointy green head, knot

the tie around my scaly neck, grasp the briefcase tightly in my claws, and start for the front door.

"You look very nice, honey," Mom says. "Your tie's a little crooked." I lean down and she adjusts the knot. "Happy Halloween." She kisses me on the top of my snout. "May your day be frightening and your night even worse." Then she hands me my traditional bag of "witch on a broomstick" cookies, and I am out the door.

I have to walk to school by myself because Sam and Lucille and I still aren't speaking to each other. I'd better make Bandito today, or there won't be anybody left to go trick-or-treating with this afternoon. I had a better Halloween the time I had my tonsils removed and Mom put me to bed and made me eat ice cream all day.

There are realistic plastic bats glued all over the front door of Stevenson Middle School today. The lobby is decorated to look like a pumpkin patch, with rows of cornstalks on stands and cloth crows hanging from the ceiling on white thread. The recorded sounds of moaning ghosts and clanking chains play over the loudspeaker. This year's decorations committee has outdone itself. Kids are milling around showing off their costumes, waiting for the first-period bell to ring.

Larry Wykoff comes running up to me. He is dressed like an enormous fly. "I need advice, Drinkwater."

"What's the problem?" I ask.

"Rachel's mad at him and he's falling apart," Dirk Schlissel says as he ambles over, balancing a volleyball on his nose. He and Dack are dressed like twin gondoliers.

"I am not falling apart," Larry protests. "I'm just a little concerned, that's all. I took your advice, Drinkwater. It's not working."

"What do you mean?" I say, trying desperately to remember exactly what advice I gave him.

"I haven't e-mailed or texted Rachel for a day and a half," he says. "And then yesterday I didn't walk her home after school. But I don't think it's making her insecure. I think it's making her mad."

"Yeah. Last night she told him she hated him more than bad breath," Dack says, grabbing the volleyball from his brother and trying to balance it on his own nose. "I'm never going to get the hang of this." His gondolier's hat falls off.

"You're driving me crazy with that thing." Larry grabs the volleyball out of Dack's hands.

Rachel Klempner approaches us. She is dressed like

a giant spider. She looks really angry. "Quick. What do I do?" Larry asks.

"Ignore her," I reply.

"Really? Are you sure this is what you did with your old girlfriend when you wanted her to shape up?" Larry looks confused.

"Oh yeah. Absolutely," I reply confidently. I don't have an old girlfriend and I never did. I have hopped on board the lying train again. "It drove Jessica Goldfrank crazy. And it's working with Rachel. I can see it in her eyes." I lower my voice. "Whatever you do, keep her on the defensive."

"Keep who on the defensive?" Rachel snaps at me.

"We were just saying how much we like your Halloween costume," I say.

"No you weren't," she says. "You were talking about me. I'm not stupid. What are you supposed to be, anyway?"

"A human," I reply.

"It's not working," she says.

"Hi, Rache," Larry says.

"Don't 'hi, Rache' me, Laurence Wykoff. I'm not speaking to you." She storms off angrily, flapping all of her eight legs as she goes.

"Come back, Rache! I miss you!" He runs off and tries to catch up to her.

I trudge upstairs to Miss Benson's social studies class on the third floor, past a sea of angels and devils and pirates and hobbits. When the bell rings I take my seat and try to look interested, but all I can think of is *Did I make Bandito?* And *Will I ever have any friends again for the rest of my life?*

Amy Armstrong sits in the row next to me. She wears a long black dress, a fake fur dalmatian coat, and a black wig with a big white stripe running through it. Of course. She's Cruella de Vil. I look over at her hopefully, but she just stares back at me blankly.

Lucille sits on my other side. Sam stands next to her. He can't sit down in his Humpty Dumpty costume. They both pretend they don't see me. I pretend I don't see them. I stew about how unfair they are being for the entire period, and when the bell finally rings, I get up to leave, whack Sam with my tail by mistake, and nearly crack his egg open. I would apologize except I'm not speaking to him.

His nose ring goes flying off and lands on my hat. It's really embarrassing. Lucille and I pretend we don't notice. I lean way down and Lucille has to fish around for it. When she finds it she hands it back to him. Sam turns bright red, turns away, puts it back in his nose, and then walks away like nothing happened.

I head downstairs to Mrs. Adams's English class. Mr. Arkady sees me coming and glides across the hallway. He is dressed as Count Dracula. I guess he doesn't realize he already looks exactly like him. He wears plastic vampire fangs, fake eyebrows, and large plastic bat wings on his shoulders. It's like wearing a costume on top of a costume. "How are you doink today, young man?" he asks.

"Great, Mr. Arkady," I say.

"Really?" he asks. He fixes me intently in his penetrating Transylvanian gaze. "You don't look so hot. You look like you could use anudder Tums."

"I'm okay. Sort of. No, I'm not," I admit. "Actually I'm feeling really stressed."

"Sometink is boddering you?" As strange as he is, Mr. Arkady is a really good listener.

"Yeah. Something is bothering me. A lot. I find out if I made Banditoes today, and I can't take the pressure any longer. Plus basically everybody I know hates my guts."

He adjusts his plastic fangs before he speaks. "Listen close, Charlie: ven I vas a little kid in Transylvania I vasn't so popular myself. I vas short. And very shy. I didn't play sports like all the udder boys in my class. I just loved science. And doink experiments. I vas a big old, how you say, 'nurt.'"

"You were a nerd? Wow. I had no idea."

"I vas big nurt. No-buddy liked me. I had big parties but no-buddy is commink. I vas unhappy all the time. My mudder vas smart. She told me, 'Little Bela, you vurry too much about vut udder pipple think about you. It is loosink battle.'"

"I know what you mean, Mr. Arkady. Lucille always says I care way too much about what other people think of me."

"Lucille, she is vun smart cookie. Vy do you care vut those Banditoes think, anyvay? If you get a bunch of fools to like you, vut have you really gotten? You must like yourself. That is vut is important. Do you understand vut I am sayink?"

"I think so, Mr. Arkady."

"Good. Now beat it. You are on provisional reentry. You must not be late for your classes. Shoo."

"Tanks for taking the time to talk to me, Mr. Arkady," I say. "I mean thanks."

"You're velcome, Charlie. Good-bye." He swirls his cape dramatically around his shoulders and glides up the stairs, back to his lair.

I turn to go and nearly crash into Amy Armstrong.

"I bet you're wondering if you made Bandito, aren't you?" she asks.

"It crossed my mind." Translation: I am so fixated on making Bandito I can barely see straight. Ever since I got voted "least likely to get invited on a playdate" in second grade in an informal but nonetheless devastating lower-school poll, I have craved the acceptance of any group of people that doesn't want me in it. Which is basically my entire class except Sam and Lucille. And my teachers. For a multidimensional character, I can sometimes be incredibly shallow.

"We're sworn to secrecy," Amy Armstrong continues. "But I'll give you a hint: you didn't make it. Somebody blackballed you. We vote by secret ballot so I can't tell you who did it. But here's a clue: Craig Dieterly."

"I thought two people had to blackball you," I say quietly.

"They did," Amy Armstrong replies. "Wykoff just flipped."

Whoa. I thought Larry Wykoff and I were friends. We enjoy hanging out together and we share common interests. Like stand-up comics and *Star Trek* and a fear of domineering women.

"Does that mean I'm never going to get to be . . ." I can't bring myself to finish my sentence. I wanted to be a Bandito so badly. My throat gets all tight and I feel like crying.

"It's not over," Amy Armstrong explains. "Any candidate who is blackballed can undo the blackball by demonstrating, quote, exceptional interest in becoming a member. End quote. You will be given one chance to redeem yourself and become a Bandito."

"What do I have to do?"

"It's simple." Amy Armstrong chuckles. "As proof of your undying loyalty to the brotherhood of Bandito you must bring us Sam's nose ring and Lucille's training bra. Such proof of loyalty will be displayed to all members, and then burned in Rachel Klempner's mother's pizza oven at the stroke of midnight."

"But . . . but . . ." I stammer.

"But what?" Amy Armstrong asks.

"Sam doesn't want anyone to know it's removable. He pretends it's real."

"Like everybody doesn't already know." Amy Armstrong taps her foot impatiently.

"And Lucille hates her training bra. I'm not even supposed to know she *wears* one." I only heard about it because her mom told my mom how she hates gym on account of everybody always teases her about it. "What you're asking me is . . . I just can't . . . I mean . . . you're asking me to . . ."

"We're asking you to do something incredibly difficult. Yes. We know." Amy Armstrong casually smooths down a wisp of stray hair. "If it was easy it wouldn't be much of a loyalty test, would it? I mean if we told you to bring us a Ritz cracker and your dog's used toothbrush, what would that prove?"

"Nothing, I guess. I just didn't expect . . ."

"You just didn't expect you'd have to work so hard to become a member. Tough toenails. What do you say, Charlie?" Amy Armstrong tilts her head to one side. "Do you have what it takes to become a Bandito?" She looks up at me through her big black lashes and smiles innocently.

Once again I have been Tasered in the head by the secret weapon that is Amy Armstrong's smile. Without even thinking about what I am getting myself into, I exclaim, "YES!!!!!!!!!!"

20
BIG DEAL

IT IS RECESS and I am waiting for the second-floor hallway to clear out, so I can break into Lucille's locker without anybody seeing me and then go steal Sam's nose ring.

What am I, some kind of hardened criminal? The force field of Amy Armstrong's smile is starting to weaken, and I am beginning to feel stupid.

Uh-oh. Here comes Mr. Arkady gliding down the hall toward me. He's bound to wonder why I am standing all by myself staring at Lucille's locker. I open my notebook and pretend to be working on a difficult math problem so I won't look suspicious. "If x is equal to the square root of pi," I mumble, "then y is equal to the sum of . . ."

"Alvays studyink, Mr. Drinkvater. Mark my vurds. You vill go far." Yeah, straight to the penitentiary if I keep this up. He glides into the teachers' lounge.

The second he is out of sight I start picking Lucille's lock with my claw. I've got to get this over with quickly and get out of here.

I can't get the door open. It's stuck. I make a lousy criminal.

Uh-oh. More footsteps. I spot Craig Dieterly at the other end of the hall, approaching Principal Muchnick's office. He's wearing leather riding boots and a black hooded overcoat. His face is covered by a white skeleton mask, and he carries a large plastic scythe. He's the grim reaper. Like he didn't already scare me enough when he was just plain old Craig Dieterly.

I try to flatten myself against the wall behind a row of lockers. My tail sticks out, and so does my big, round belly. But Dieterly is far too intent on breaking into Principal Muchnick's office to notice me.

He takes out a paper clip and fiddles with the lock. In a minute the door swings open, and he slips into the office like a professional cat burglar. He makes a much better criminal than I do.

What in the world is Craig Dieterly doing breaking and entering on school property?

It isn't until I see him sneaking out again a minute later with a thick manila file under his arm that it dawns on me: he's got my transcript in there. My whole life reduced to a few dozen pages of cold hard facts— my grades; Dr. Craverly's psychological evaluation; my teachers' reports; and . . . just shoot me now and be done with it . . . my entire, legal signature. Charles **ELMER** Drinkwater.

If Craig Dieterly tells everyone my dreaded middle name, I will never ever get to be a Bandito. Period. End of sentence. *Finito.*

Just then Sam and Lucille come running up to Craig Dieterly. "We've been watching you," Sam says. "We saw you break into that office."

"Out of my way, Fat Face," he says.

"What are you doing with Charlie's transcript, Dieterly?" Lucille asks.

"I'm going to find his middle name in there, and when I do I will tell every single person I can find. And if anyone was even *thinking* of talking to him. Or hanging out with him. Or becoming friends with him. They won't anymore." Craig Dieterly chuckles ominously. "Now move it or lose it."

"We're telling Principal Muchnick on you," Sam says.

"You do and you're toast," Craig Dieterly says.

"That's our friend's private property," Lucille says. "You won't get away with this!"

And then she and Sam grab Craig Dieterly by the arm and try to stop him from going up the stairs. But he just flicks them aside like ants and runs for the stairs.

All of a sudden it hits me like a ton of bricks, and I come crashing to my senses. Like when Sleeping Beauty wakes up after the prince kisses her. Only I am not Sleeping Beauty. And if a prince ever kisses me I will bop him on the head with my tail.

What have I been thinking? My two best friends are willing to risk the wrath of Craig Dieterly for me, and here I am about to steal their stuff so I can be a member of a clique that they're not even allowed to join? I must have been out of my mind. How low can a mutant dinosaur sink?

I hurry over and help Sam and Lucille up. "Are you okay?" I ask.

"Yeah. We're fine," Lucille says as she rearranges her meter maid costume. "Let's get out of here, Sam."

"I saw what you did, guys," I start. "And it was—"

"We didn't know you were watching," Sam interrupts. "C'mon, Lucille."

"It was awesome," I say.

"No big whup," Lucille says.

"Common courtesy," Sam says. "No more, no less." My two friends start to leave.

"Hold your horses, guys," I say. "You came to my rescue after I treated you like used belly button lint. You are the best and truest friends a creature could ever have. Even if you never forgive me, I want you to know that I am deeply sorry for the way I treated you. And I apologize. I have been acting like a complete and total idiot."

"You most certainly have," Sam says.

"You know, turning into a creature is one thing, Charlie," Lucille says. "But forgetting who your real friends are is quite another."

"You're right," I say.

"Of course she's right, you knucklehead!" Sam exclaims. "And don't you ever do it again. Now don't just stand there twiddling your claws, pal, you go after Dieterly and we'll find Principal Muchnick."

"Roger, wilco, over and out!" I run off to find Craig Dieterly. I am so relieved to have my best friends back you couldn't wipe the smile off my face if you tried. If I had a face. And a mouth. And lips.

"He's nothing but a two-faced, backstabbing, troublemaking, no-good lizard," Rachel Klempner says. She's standing in the middle of the pumpkin patch in the lobby, surrounded by cornstalks and crows. She's talking to Amy Armstrong and holding hands with Larry Wykoff. The two lovebirds have finally patched it up.

I should have known: Larry Wykoff blackballed me because Rachel Klempner made him. When she sees me she doesn't even skip a beat. "Great to see you, Charlie. Happy Halloween."

"Where's Dieterly?" I brush the fake cobwebs from my hat.

"What are you supposed to be, Drinkwater, an accountant or something?" Craig Dieterly says. He emerges from behind a large tombstone. I see my folder under his arm. I hope he hasn't opened it yet.

"A human being," I reply. "Which is more than I can say for you."

"Prepare to get squashed, Big Bug," Craig Dieterly snarls. He puts down his scythe and rolls up his sleeves. Ghosts moan and chains clank over the PA system.

I tap Amy Armstrong gently on the shoulder with my claw. "What's up?" she asks.

Dirk and Dack Schlissel, in their twin gondolier costumes, and Alice Pincus, in her Little Miss Muffet outfit come by to see what's going on. So does Norm Swerling. He looks just like Harry Potter.

"I've decided not to take you up on your generous offer, Amy," I say.

"What!" Amy Armstrong exclaims.

"Thanks, but no thanks," I reply. "I don't really want to be a Bandito after all." Mr. Arkady was right. If you get a bunch of fools to like you, what do you really have?

"You ungrateful little nothing!" Amy fumes.

"Batten down your hatches, Smelly Reptile Guy," Craig Dieterly growls. "There's a big storm heading your way. And I'm not talking about the weather." He starts flexing his muscles and walking slowly toward me. A bunch of middle-schoolers dressed like witches and goblins come over to watch.

Sam and Lucille run in breathlessly. "Principal Muchnick says he'll be here in a minute," Sam pants.

"Are you telling me you'd rather be friends with a couple of terminal losers?" Amy shrieks.

"Sam and Lucille aren't terminal losers. They're my best friends," I say. "They're better and smarter and nicer than all of you Banditoes and One-Upsters put together." The crowd murmurs excitedly. Sam and Lucille are beaming.

"I must have been out of my mind when I brought you up for membership!" Amy Armstrong exclaims. "You're the same old forgettable Charlie Drinkwater you always were. Only now you have webbed feet and a tail. You couldn't be a Bandito if your life depended on it."

"I'm glad, because if the earth was about to explode and the only spaceship capable of interplanetary travel was evacuating in five minutes and Banditoes were on it, I wouldn't even buy a ticket."

Sam and Lucille look at me, brimming with pride, and I look gratefully back at them, until I notice Craig

Dieterly closing in on me like an armed tank on a mission.

"Take it back right now, Mothra, or prepare to meet your maker." Craig flicks me on the side of my big green head with his finger.

"I really wish you wouldn't do that," I say. "Fighting doesn't solve anything."

"Yeah, but it's so much fun," Craig Dieterly replies. "Listen up, Slimola: first I am going to tear you into little pieces. And then when you are squirming on the ground and begging for mercy, I will hit you with your middle name. A blow from which you will never recover." Craig Dieterly grabs my shirt in his fist and pulls me toward him, twisting my collar so tightly I can barely breathe. "Don't you ever say bad things about me and my friends again. Understand?"

"Yes," I whisper hoarsely.

"I can't hear you," he says.

"That's because . . . you're . . . choking me," I gasp. He lets go of my shirt and I stagger back against a papier-mâché ghost standing in front of a large mausoleum.

"Apologize. Now. Say you didn't mean it, Drink-water." He pulls back his brawny arm and prepares to punch me in the snout. "Or else."

Mom's wish is coming true. I am having a very frightening day. This is one Halloween I will never forget.

"I won't take it back!" I exclaim. "I meant what I said. And you can hit me as hard as you want to, I'll still mean it. Banditoes and One-Upsters are nasty and boring and selfish. I'm glad I'm not like you." The words are out of my mouth before I even realize what I am saying. I couldn't stop myself if I tried.

"Take that!" I close my eyes and swing my powerful claw as hard as I can in Craig Dieterly's direction and miss him completely. Instead, I catch on to the side of his shirt and rip it in two places.

Now I've really done it. Not only will Dieterly cream me, Principal Muchnick will suspend me quicker than you can say "mutant dinosaurs attacking their fellow students on school property is so against the rules it isn't funny." Forget Harvard. I wouldn't even get into Southern Illinois Vocational at this point.

Craig Dieterly turns red and his neck starts to bulge out like someone is pumping helium into it. You can practically see the steam coming out of his ears. "You hit me. I have witnesses. Now you've really done it, Shrimpboats!" he shouts. "Stand back, everyone!"

I cringe and close my hooded eyelids tightly. I bury my head in my claws. Suddenly a voice cries "**STOP!!!**" I look up and see Dave racing up the stairs like Superman. "Don't lay a hand on my little brother," he shouts, "or you'll have me to deal with, Dieterly!"

Craig Dieterly takes one look at my brother and puts his arm down immediately. "Charlie and I were just horsing around."

"It didn't look like horsing around to me." Dave comes over and puts an arm on my shoulder. "I came over to apologize to you, Charlie. Looks like I got here just in the nick of time. Are you all right?"

"Thanks to you," I say gratefully.

"You don't have to thank me, Charlie," Dave says. "That's what big brothers are for. Dad set me straight this morning. He's says I've been so busy thinking about myself I didn't even consider what this week must have been like for you. He's right, Charlie. I'm really sorry. I've been acting like a selfish idiot."

"I'm pretty familiar with that sort of thing myself," I say.

Principal Muchnick pushes his way through rows of cornstalks as he storms into the lobby. He hits his head on a hanging crow. He doesn't look happy.

"You got here just in time, Principal Muchnick," Craig Dieterly says. "Look what this violent creature did to me." He holds up his torn shirt.

"What are you carrying under your arm, Dieterly?" Principal Muchnick asks.

"Charlie Drinkwater's transcript, sir," Craig Dieterly says.

"I thought so. That's private property. Where'd you get it, Mr. Dieterly?"

"Drinkwater stole it from your office, sir," Craig Dieterly lies. "I was about to return it. Cross my heart and hope to die."

"No, you weren't. You stole it yourself," Sam says. "We saw him do it, Principal Muchnick."

"We took pictures of him with our phones," Lucille adds. "He's lying and we can prove it. Want to see?"

"Shut up, losers!" Craig Dieterly yells.

"No. You shut up, Mr. Dieterly. Give it here," Principal Muchnick orders. "Right now." Craig Dieterly gnashes his teeth and hands him my transcript. "I have had enough trouble out of you to last a lifetime. You hear me?"

"Yes, sir." Craig Dieterly looks down sullenly.

"What do you have to say for yourself, Mr. Drinkwater?"

"First I would like to thank my real true friends for standing up for me. And then I'd like to say a special word of gratitude to Mr. Arkady for his continued inspiration and—"

"No, no, no, that's not what I meant," Principal Muchnick interrupts. "Who started it?"

All eyes are on me as I take a deep breath and confess. "I did, Principal Muchnick. I started the whole thing."

"You did?" Principal Muchnick is amazed. "Really?"

"Yes. I threw the first punch," I answer. "I'm not proud of myself. I don't approve of violence in conflict resolution, and if I had to do it again . . ."

"Be quiet," Principal Muchnick says. "You finally stood up for yourself. It's a miracle. I never thought I'd live to see the day. Congratulations, Mr. Drinkwater, you are no longer on provisional reentry. Consider yourself officially matriculated."

Craig Dieterly picks up his scythe and smashes it against the wall.

"As for you, Mr. Dieterly," Principal Muchnick says,

"you can collect your belongings and see me in my office in ten minutes. You just got yourself a two-day suspension for breaking and entering, not to mention stealing. Not to mention lying to a school official under oath."

"I'm so proud of you I'm speechless, little bro," Dave says. He hugs me as hard as he can.

Then Sam and Lucille and I jump up and down wildly and give each other the official Mainframe handshake. "All for one and one for all!" I am so happy I feel like my heart is going to burst.

21
SUGAR SHOCK

WE'VE BEEN TRICK-OR-TREATING for close to three hours, and our pillowcases are nearly full. My uncle opens the door to his split-level ranch house and looks curiously at me, Lucille, and Sam. "Who are you supposed to be, Lucille?" Uncle Marvin prides himself on his great Halloween costumes. This year he's Shrek. Last year he was Dolly Parton.

"I'm a meter maid, Mr. O'Connor." Lucille points out the parking tickets pinned to her blouse. "Can't you tell?"

"Oh yeah, now that you mention it," Uncle Marvin replies. "Very subtle." He dumps a fistful of M&M's Pretzel bags into each of our pillowcases.

"Who do you think I am, sir?" Sam shows off his Humpty Dumpty costume for Uncle Marvin. "I'll give you a hint—I fell off a wall."

"Uh . . . One of the Three Stooges, maybe?" Uncle Marvin squints and scratches his head.

"I'm Humpty Dumpty," Sam says indignantly. "I look just like him. Everybody thinks so."

"You do. You look just like him, Sam. I don't know what I was thinking." Uncle Marvin turns his attention to me. His jaw drops and he breathes heavily through his open mouth. "Now there's a Creature from the Black Lagoon if I ever saw one!" he exclaims.

"I'm supposed to be a human, Uncle Marvin," I explain. "That's how come I'm wearing a hat and a tie and carrying a briefcase."

"Of course you are," Uncle Marvin says, and then calls into the house, "Your nephew's here, honey!"

He stands back as my mom's sister, Harriet, races to the door. Short, extremely fat, and naturally rather ogreish herself; she makes a very believable Princess Fiona,

Shrek's true love. It takes her a moment to catch her breath.

"My goodness, Charlie, let me take a good look at you!" she pants. "Oh my. Doris was right, Marv, the family resemblance is startling." She comes over and gives me a big hug. "You're the spitting image of your grandmother, bless her soul. Isn't he, Marv?" She takes out a handkerchief and dabs at her eyes. She looks like she's about to bawl. I guess crying sort of runs in the family.

"He sure does, Harriet. Say, would you kids like to come in for donuts and hot mulled cider?" Uncle Marvin asks.

"We'd love to, Uncle Marvin, but we haven't finished trick-or-treating yet, and I promised Mom we'd be home by seven." I wave a reluctant good-bye with my tail, and the three of us head off in search of more candy.

Sheets made into ghosts and tied to lampposts flap in the wind. Silhouettes of witches on broomsticks float across windows. We fill our satchels with bags of Moose Munch and chocolate-covered raisins at Mrs. Pagliuso's house. "I like your costume, Charlie," she says.

"Do you know what I am, Mrs. Pagliuso?"

"I sure do," she says. "You're a human being. You've

been one all along, underneath those claws and flippers,
I guess."

"Thanks, Mrs. P.," I say. Looks like she's not afraid
of me anymore. As we turn to leave, a few fifth-graders
dressed as C-3PO, Jabba the Hutt, and Darth Vader approach the house. No one asks for my autograph. Or
tries to touch my tail. Or takes pictures of me with their
phones.

Tonight I'm just another teenager trying to fit in.
One more alien, swimming in a sea of scary creatures. It
was fun and exciting to be the new creature on the block.
But being yesterday's news is a lot less stressful.

"Better get to bed, Charlie," Mom yells from upstairs.
"It's almost midnight."

"I'll be up in a few minutes, Mom," I yell back. "I
promise." Sam and Lucille have gone home and I am
watching the last few minutes of *Creature from the
Black Lagoon*. We didn't make it all the way through the
movie because after dinner we played Bananagrams and
didn't sit down to watch until after ten.

"'Night, Charlie," Dave says as he pokes his head
into the den. He just got back from Janie Belzer's house.

"Again?" he asks, pointing at the TV. "Can't we find you something else to watch?"

"Are you kidding? I love this movie." I hold on tightly to the clicker.

"Yeah, but how many times have you seen it?" he asks.

"Not enough," I reply.

Dave hands me a small framed drawing. "Janie asked me to give you this. She worked on it all week."

"Thanks," I say as I take it in my claws. I study the picture carefully. This is me. Forever. Those are my scales. My claws. My tail. My fangs are pretty scary. So are the spiky ridges along my sloping forehead. But there's a mischievous glint in my eyes. And my jaws turn up a little at the edges. If you look really closely you can tell that I am smiling. It will never be a human face. But as mutant dinosaurs go, it's not a bad face. "Janie did a really good job," I say at last.

"I thought so," Dave says.

"How are you guys doing?" I set the picture carefully on the coffee table, next to the picture of me and Dave when we went to Epcot a couple of years ago. "I was worried that maybe things were still . . . you know . . . a little rocky . . . on account of me."

"We're cool. Janie drew a portrait of me, and I sent her flowers."

"I'm glad."

"What's the monster doing to her now?" Dave asks, pointing at the television set.

"He's not a monster, Dave, he's a creature. There's a big difference. Monsters hurt people for no reason. Creatures are basically friendly but if you hurt them they'll fight back. So the *creature* has abducted the beautiful Kay Lawrence and taken her to his lair in the cavern. In a few minutes Dr. Maia, Dr. Reed, and Lucas are going to shoot him with their rifles."

"Doesn't sound like a very happy ending."

"No. But it's very exciting." Balthazar walks in and barks a gentle hello. "Up, Bally, up," I say. Balthazar hops onto the couch with me. He roots around in the cushions with his big brown nose and licks up stray bits of potato chip that have fallen in between. When he is satisfied there aren't any left he puts his big brown shaggy head on my lap and sighs contentedly.

Dave and I both watch the movie for a minute.

"I'm glad you're my brother," Dave says simply.

"Me too," I say. He smiles, and then goes upstairs to get ready for bed.

I turn my attention back to the TV. The creature has just been shot. He roars with pain and thrashes around in the jungle until he finds his lagoon. This part always gets me. But tonight his death seems especially poignant. I hold my ears and look away as he falls into the dark abyss.

What's that? I hear footsteps outside the window. Balthazar suddenly growls, and my knees grow weak. He presses his shivering body tightly to my side. I turn off the light next to the couch so I can see better. *Click.*

It isn't a shadow. Shadows don't move, and whatever this is, it's definitely moving. I can scarcely catch my breath as I watch a large, shapeless hulk inching from the big evergreen next to the driveway to the bushes near the side of the house.

Of course. It's Sam. I should have known. He went and put on a new costume and came back to terrify me. I bet Lucille put him up to it. "It's just Sam, Balthazar. Or Craig Dieterly. That's it. It's Dieterly. He's returned to teach me a lesson. Let's hope he goes away quickly, Bally." I wait, motionless, listening for a sign of life from the lawn. I hear nothing but the rustling of leaves in the wind, and some kids giggling in the distance.

And then all of a sudden a car passes and lights up the lawn for a second in the glare of its headlights. I catch a glimpse of two powerful jaws and a pair of dark hooded eyes gleaming back at me in the moonlight. I'm about to scream . . . but then I realize I'm just looking at a reflection of myself in the window. Like my dad always says, if you have a vivid imagination and you go around watching scary movies before you go to bed, you have to be prepared for that sort of thing.

"I'm going to bed, Bally." It's so late that I'm starting to imagine things. Balthazar hops off the couch and follows me upstairs to my room, never leaving my side, while I brush my fangs and get into my pj's. After I've arranged my covers and squeezed myself into bed, Balthazar jumps up and snuggles peacefully in the crook of my claws.

Mom comes in to give me a good-night hug, and my dad joins her as they wait for me to fall asleep. "I'm not tired, guys," I say.

"That's because you ate too much sugar," Dad says.

"I had a really frightening day, Mom. And my night was even worse." I laugh and I hear Dave stirring.

"Keep it down over there," my brother complains.

"Sorry, Dave," I whisper. "I'll shut up. I didn't mean to..." My brother is snoring loudly before I have a chance to finish my sentence.

"You just think calm, pleasant thoughts, honey," Mom says. "It's been a long, hard week."

I try to keep my eyes open, but when your dog is snuggling in your claws ... and your mother is stroking your cranial ridge ... and your father is singing "A Hundred Bottles of Beer on the Wall" ... and your big brother is snoring loudly in the next bed ... it's hard for a seventh-grade creature to stay up for very long.

And before you can say, "I have already had enough adventures to last me for one lifetime and I'm not even halfway through with my story," I am fast asleep.

THE DRINKWATER FAMILY

ACKNOWLEDGMENTS

To Joy Peskin and everyone at Viking/Penguin for their unwavering support and encouragement. With special thanks to my editor, Leila Sales, for her wisdom and invaluable advice.

Lee Salem

BOB BALABAN is the author of the popular Mc-
Growl series. He was inspired to write *The Creature from the
Seventh Grade* because when he was twelve he was something of a creature himself. As he puts it: "I was the shortest,
skinniest kid in my class. I wore braces and big black glasses
with Coke-bottle thick lenses, and my hobbies were making
dioramas and learning Irish folk dances. I didn't have scales
and an eight-foot tail, but I might as well have."

When he is not writing children's books, Bob acts, di-
rects, and produces. He produced and costarred in the Acad-
emy Award–winning movie *Gosford Park* and has been nom-
inated for a few Emmys, some Screen Actors Guild awards,
four Golden Globes, and a Tony award. He has appeared in
nearly a hundred movies.

Bob is happy to call Bridgehampton, New York, his home.

Jennifer Rash

ANDY RASH

(www.rashworks.com) has illustrated many books by fine authors like Mr. Balaban, and has also written and illustrated several books of his own, including *Ten Little Zombies: A Love Story* and *Are You a Horse?* His award-winning illustration work has appeared in *Fortune, The New York Times, The New Yorker, Time, The Wall Street Journal,* and *Wired,* among others. He lives in Milwaukee with his wife and son.